CRINKLES AND OTHER STORIES

MICHAEL RYDER

Thomas Publishing

COPYRIGHT

"This Time, I Return for Good" was published originally in *Fiction River: Time Streams* (2013).

"X-Cal" was published originally in *Penumbra* (2015).

"Evil and Abigail Carr" was published originally in *Devilfish Review* (2015).

"Crinkles" was published originally in *Compelling Science Fiction* (2016).

Sign up for Michael Ryder's email newsletter

Get an email update when a new Michael Ryder book is ready. You can unsubscribe at any time with one click.

Sign up at AuthorMichaelRyder.com

In memory of my father

CONTENTS

INTRODUCTION

How does one introduce one's first collection of short fiction? Does one distance oneself from potential awkwardness by referring to oneself as "one"? Does one humbly profess one's surprise and delight at one's stories being selected for publication by the discerning editors of leading magazines of short fiction? Does one wax philosophical about overarching themes or cultural resonances that one detects in one's own stories? Does one inevitably take the "one" schtick one sentence too far?

Perhaps instead I can I share a bit about these stories. The lead tale, "This Time, I Return for Good," is the outcome of an intensive writing workshop on the Oregon coast in the spring of 2013. I arrived a new writer, riddled with doubt, worried I lacked the chops to be there. When the instructor handed out our first assignment — in two days!

write a short story! about time travel! — to say I knew fear would be an understatement. I knew big fear. Huge fear. Shock and fear. Bewilderment and fear. Despair and fear. Fear and more fear. Fear because I was a fraud. A phony. I didn't belong with this group of experienced, dedicated, talented writers. I hadn't written short fiction since college. The notion that I could write a story in two days? Around a topic I knew nothing about? Absurd!

Yet somehow I did. Funny how fear folds under pressure. The story came from nowhere. For two nights, the words flowed. I'll always be grateful to the instructor for opening my eyes to a grand new universe of fictional possibility.

"X-Cal," the second story in this collection, happened because a writer friend (from the Oregon workshop) pointed me toward a magazine seeking stories about Arthurian legend. I'm not a Renaissance Fair kind of guy — jousting and fair maidens ain't my cuppa, if you get my drift — so I almost passed. But then I thought: What if I transported King Arthur and Gwendolyn and Merlin and Lancelot and the Knights of the Round Table to a tech startup in present-day Oakland, California?

Sure, count me in!

I have no idea how "Evil and Abigail Carr" came to be. The story just happened. It's the only monster story I've written, and the first mystery story. Its origins may lie in my enjoyment of Victorian murder-mysteries. Or maybe I was just in a bad mood?

"The Noises in the Wall" takes place over the course of twenty minutes in the life of a young man who may or may not be, to use the clinical term, koo-koo ga-ga. You'll have to decide.

"Smile" is about a guy in San Francisco who accidentally destroys Alcatraz while working up the courage to ask a cute girl on a date. A note to the authorities: This story is *pure fiction*.

"Crinkles," the anchor story in this collection, is an optimistic take on artificial intelligence. The pessimistic view, a common meme of late, makes for great "us vs. them" fiction. But in this story, I chose to explore what happens when an AI ends up liking us.

How does one end one's introduction to one's first collection of short fiction? With something like this:

I hope you enjoy these stories.

MICHAEL RYDER

SAN FRANCISCO, CA

OCTOBER 2017

THIS TIME, I RETURN FOR GOOD

Dearest Ned,

You are in your aunt's study, hiding behind the leather chair near the fire, remembering the grand adventure stories we once read to each other, me to you, you to me. The hidden alcove behind the chair is an escape, a refuge from the crowd in the house and their well-intended but thoroughly misplaced expressions of sympathy.

Your unusual vantage point allows you to see an envelope, with your name on it, pinned to the back of the chair.

You tear the letter open and read it with joy in your heart, for you know it is from me. Yet what you read puzzles you. Eagerness turns to suspicion. You wonder how anyone can know what is on these pages, because knowing what this letter knows is impossible. You fear it is a joke, a malicious prank, an attempt to mock what you so firmly believe. How dare they, you think. Part of you is tempted to hurl the letter into the fire, to watch its words, its instructions, shrivel to ash.

I know this because you tell me. You tell me in four days.

I know this confuses you, my son. I ask for your patience, until I explain.

This is what you do. Tomorrow, when the clock in the hall strikes noon, you take this letter to your aunt. She is preparing to leave for an appointment, adjusting her hair in the mirror near the front door. You tell her she must read this letter right away. She looks at you with compassion and concern — oh, she loves you so! — but says she must meet the lawyer to review final arrangements for the estate, and will return as quickly as she can.

But she does not leave. She stays. She stays because you show her this letter.

Remember, my son, when the clock strikes noon.

With all my love,
Your father

My dearest Susan,

You are worried about being late for the appointment, and vexed at Mr. Lapham for insisting on meeting so soon after the funeral. You do not want to be away from Ned, for he worries you terribly. His refusal to grieve is unbalanced, you fear, and his insistence I am alive, unhealthy. You fear his stubborn denial of my passing will only cause greater pain when, as it must, the truth can no longer be ignored.

This letter concerns you deeply. You do not trust it and do not understand it. But Ned is so insistent, so firm, so very desperate for your support, that you, despite your doubts, place a call to Mr. Lapham. You tell him you will have to meet him tomorrow instead.

Much to your surprise, he is angry and alarmed, unusually so, given how respectfully he's handled his relations with you until now. But today he is demanding and short. He says the details are essential. He insists the meeting must be right away.

You tell him no, and hang up the telephone. You tremble for a moment. You usually take pains to be agreeable. Your firmness of manner is out of character. You attribute that to your own grief, and to your fears for Ned's state of mind.

I know this because you tell me. You tell me in three days.

Please know that I explain everything.

This is what you do. You walk into the kitchen and tell the cook and the cleaning girl to take the night off. In the basement, you open the hidden door to the storm cellar where you and I once played. Inside the storm cellar, you move the new shelf and reveal the door to the secret safe room I built without your knowledge. You cut the cord of the telephone, turn off the lights throughout the house, and ignore the knocks at the door. Shortly before ten o'clock, you take Ned into the safe room. You do not use candles or lanterns of any kind. Instead, you guide yourselves by touch. You pull the shelf tight until it fully covers the safe room door. You hear the men break in and move through the house. You and Ned remain silent. The men search the basement, but they do not find the door behind the shelf. Shortly after midnight, angry and frustrated, the men leave.

In the morning, you go upstairs and, with Ned, restore the house to its normal state of affairs.

At the stroke of noon, you take this letter to Mr. Lapham.

With all my love,
Your adoring younger brother,
Benjamin

Eric,

As my sister hands you this letter, you are painfully aware of the curiosity and caution at war on my sister's face. You understand she no longer fully trusts you.

You turn away because she must not see your anger. She must not see you calculating whether she, this woman you secretly love, can be manipulated, used, to get to me.

You do not know if you still have the will, the fortitude, to use her. You worry you have found your reason to stop flowing.

You fear what happens if you stop flowing. You know that only one person — you — has even the barest chance of finding me. You know you must find me, because what happens if, against all odds, consequences be damned, I succeed? Already I've betrayed you — sacrificed our partnership to plunge recklessly, dangerously, into my impossible quest. It is easy to imagine that I am capable of much worse.

I know the pity you feel, tinged with contempt, for me, your former comrade-in-arms, your former best friend, who stood with you, times and again, to fight the good fights, but who fell, hollowed by tragedy, into a haunted husk of his better self, consumed by visions of a time, a flow, that cannot be. I feel your sadness, my friend.

You see us that cold January morning in the American capital, quietly removing the gun from the pocket of that misguided man's coat. You hear the young president, his wife and two young daughters at his side, lifting us with his stirring speech. We linger to hear all of it, every word, though of course we shouldn't. You see the would-be assassin, thwarted by a pickpocket in his moment of infamy, raging to the heavens. You also see, in the days that follow, the man's hatred melt away. You see him, much to his surprise, sob with relief.

You see us retrieve the piece of paper in Alan Turing's study, after the wind blew it from his desk to the floor. You see us return it to the desk in the precise position needed for him, with his once-in-a-generation mind, to see it and make the critical leap — to create the code-breaking machine that saves England from the Germans. A single piece of paper, my friend. A piece of paper!

You see us assist an old woman across the street, helping her move just two seconds more quickly, preventing the bus from swerving into the railroad tracks to avoid her, preventing the bus from hitting the commuter train, preventing the deaths of so many, including a young girl named Emily Wu who, as every child is taught in school, grows up to cure diabetes.

Ours is a noble profession, Eric, an essential one. Dangerous, too, with the criminals, politicians, corporations, and foolhardy amateur explorers vying to harness the flows for their generally nefarious ends.

But we are not our profession. The time comes (oh, how that phrase charms and confounds) when we step out of the flows.

All of this goes through your mind as my sister Susan stares at you. Without warning, your face flushes red, but not because you realize you're ready to leave the flows, that you're ready to be with her.

Your face flushes because you realize something else. You see that this time, something is different. You look closely at the letter, the yellowed paper, the faint handwriting, now fading. This time, at the edge of your vision, you see the words materializing on the parchment as you read them. You realize I have found the flow. Yes, old friend, *the* flow. The single flow I left everything behind to chase, including you.

You take a step back, staggered. Even as your mind races, it refuses to accept the evidence. No one has ever done what I, apparently, have managed to do. But if I have, then others can as well. Fear surges forward, fresh and urgent, the terrible possibilities playing out.

But with the fear, too, comes hope. Yes, my friend, *hope*. Hope that I have not, in my zealotry, enabled the organized rape of time. Hope that you and Susan have a chance. Hope, even, that I, your friend who abandoned you, can rejoin the lives of his best friend, his sister, his son, and, yes, even his long-lost wife.

Yes, even Jane. I can almost hear the gasp escape your lips.

I know you have hope because you tell me. You tell me in two days.

This time, my friend, all flows as it should. This time, I return for good.

This is what you do. You flow to the Directorate and complete a task so inconceivable that, of all the agents of any and every time, only you ever pull it off: You steal all traces of you and me and our grand history and bury that history in the molten core of Krakatoa as it explodes. Simultaneously, you inform the Directorate that I am back but mad as a hatter and believe, apparently, that I can raise the dead.

At noon tomorrow, when you are summoned to meet with the Director, you place this letter in his hands.

With great love and respect,
Your friend and once-wayward partner,
Benjamin

Director,

You are surprised when Eric hands you this letter. You turn to your staff and order them out of the flow.

You ask Eric what he makes of this. You are furious, and fearful, when he says you have to read it and decide for yourself.

You prefer not to decide for yourself. Deciding for yourself is dangerous for a man in your position.

In moments like this, you fear you are not in charge. You fear control is merely an illusion. You fear this letter, which is tracking your fears with uncomfortable accuracy, will take you even deeper into your subconscious.

Your anger erupts. You ask Eric what kind of fool nonsense this is. Eric tells you the letter is from Benjamin, and to keep reading.

You frown, but you keep reading. You are taken aback when you read that I am asking you to choose between two flows.

You scoff. You say no man can isolate, let alone control, an individual flow. No man can identify, let alone control, the infinite intersections linking an individual flow with others.

Eric tells you to look at the words you are reading, as you read them, and to read them slowly. You are shocked to see, at the edge of your vision, the words being written on the page.

The same shock, the same horror felt by Eric, now courses through you. You tell Eric this must be a trick. He shakes his head.

You examine the yellowed pages, crinkled with age, and the black, faded ink, written two centuries ago, yet as new and fresh as the morning snow.

You know there is only one explanation: You know I have control of the flow.

In a panic, you rush to the window and look out upon the great city below. But you see nothing different. You rush to a mirror and see the same worn, aging face. You call your wife and ask if your daughter is coming home for Christmas. Your wife says she doubts it, given how rude you were to her new boyfriend at Thanksgiving.

You turn to Eric. Is everything the same, you

ask. He nods and says yes. He tells you he's analyzed fourteen billion trillion flows and found no new anomalies.

You say to him, You're telling me the bastard did it.

You hear Eric say, I'm telling you the bastard did it.

You wonder what I want. You begin to think like a Director. You begin to consider how my discovery might be harnessed. The various ways it might be used.

You see me cut off that line of thinking. You see the letter explain that my discovery lives and dies with me. You read that only I know how to control, isolate, and edit an individual flow. You know, deep in your bones, that I will never reveal that secret, that I have safeguards in place to ensure that.

You know I am five steps ahead of you, as I always am. You resent and hate me for that, never more so than at this moment.

You suspect the choice I am about to force on you will be painful for you. You know I loathe you. You know, if I had the option, I would smash you like the worthless bug you are. Drop you in the Amazon into a school of piranhas. Roast you alive, slowly, over an open fire. Strip away your position, your family, your reputation — anything and every-thing you hold dear. I have imagined countless punishments, all of them just, all of them richly deserved.

But understand, as you read this sentence, that I cannot exact my vengeance. Understand that my exquisite, and fragile, control of this flow requires you to be able to make a decision, of your own free will.

It is ironic that my fate, my eternal happiness, lies with you, the man who ruined the happiness I once found. Perhaps it is because the universe decrees balance — requires that in exchange for my happiness, your cowardice and greed and craven indifference go unpunished. If so, lucky you.

Your decision is between two flows, nearly identical, buffed and shined and polished to perfection. One flow survives, the other dies.

The first flow is the one you experience now. In this flow, I am a renegade, a criminal, an unhinged terrorist, threatening the safety of the universe in pursuit of a mad dream. The traps you have set for me, in London and elsewhere, are cunning and may very well succeed in capturing me, someday, sometime.

In this flow, you are the Director, head of the most powerful secret organization ever to exist. You rose to the top through merit — I grant you that willingly, given your ambition, work ethic and political savvy — but also through treachery. You feel an urge to deny the treachery, but you don't. Neither of us is a fool. We both know the terrible things you do.

In this flow, when you identified me as a rival, you set in motion a plan to remove me.

You didn't anticipate Jane. You didn't know about her, of course. I did all I could to keep her invisible from you.

You didn't know I would soon stop flowing. You didn't know your rival was exiting the arena.

You could argue — have argued — that what happened was my fault. Had I been less skillful at keeping her a secret, you contend, Jane might still be alive. In my darkest moments, I have made that argument myself.

You wonder, occasionally, what might be if Jane hadn't taken the cup of coffee intended for me, or if the poison had been, not a standard-issue cancer inducer, but rather a poison genetically tuned for me. Do you regret what happened? Do you wish the trap you set for me had been more carefully calibrated?

I expect the answer is no. To you, innocents are immaterial. An individual doesn't matter if he doesn't impact the flow.

Let us look again at that last sentence: An individual doesn't matter if he doesn't impact the flow. As the first, and only, man in all of human history to gain broad control of a flow, I have the benefit of seeing what happens within this flow. Including, Director, what happens to you.

I can tell you two things: The first is that you, Director, by your own definition, are immaterial.

You do not matter because you do not impact the flow.

You want to protest. Your ego demands it. But you know, deep down, I am right.

The second thing I can tell you is this: There is a cancer in your colon. It has spread. In four months, you will be dead.

I wish I did not have to tell you. I wish I could do nothing. I wish I could let you die.

But as I have already noted, my happiness depends on your choice.

Let me tell you about the second flow. In the second flow, except in your memories, I do not exist. Eric does not exist. Our feats, our exploits, never happened. We were never rivals. You never attempted to poison me. You never murdered Jane.

You are still the Director, still the same man, except in one tiny, crucial, respect: When you were a child, your mother took a cooking class and learned to make healthier meals for her family. You grew up eating more fruits, more vegetables. This habit continued into your adulthood.

As a consequence, the polyp in your colon has not yet turned cancerous. It will, in several years, but in this flow, you have time to treat it, to literally nip it in the bud. In this flow, you continue as Director for many more years.

You understand the choice before you. Do nothing, and die in four months.

Or, do this: You remove any and all traps set for

me or Eric. You never attempt or take, or allow or enable or suggest or in any way precipitate, any action against anyone Eric or I ever know. You lift the embargo on flows in and out of London on the third day of the sixth month in the year 1923. And you slip this letter into the mail to be delivered on this same day to Miss Jane Seeton, 14 Marylebone Way, London.

If you choose the second choice, I enable the second flow.

This is what you do. You decide now.

I remain,
Now and always,
Benjamin

June 3, 1923

Dear Miss Seeton,

Allow me to introduce myself. My name is Benjamin Burden. I am, today, a trader of spices and coffees. But five years ago, in the last months of the war, I was a captain in the U.S. Army in France and had the great pleasure of knowing your brother Charles. We became close before his death. His warmth and irrepressible cheer were a great boon to us in those dark times, and even now the memory of his laughter brings a smile to my face.

He spoke very highly of you — his devilishly

brilliant little sister, he called you — and he urged me, if ever I was in London, to pay my respects.

I am in London at present, staying at the Edgeway Hotel in Leicester Square, and I would be honored if you would allow me to meet you. This will seem presumptuous, coming as it does from a complete stranger, but I feel I already know you. I have a suspicion we will become the greatest of friends.

I look forward to your reply.

With kindest regards,

Forever in your service,

Benjamin Burden

X-CAL

The universe invests a lot of power in the small things. Believe me, I know. I learned the hard way.

The scene is this: I slowly make my way up the stairs to the third floor, stopping now and then to catch my breath. I get to 3B. Through the door's frosted glass pane, I hear the tap-tap-tap of fingers on a keyboard.

I turn the knob and push open the door, and there he is.

The kid — I guess you could call him the hero of the tale. Hunched over his laptop like a tired scarecrow, light from the screen reflecting off his pale oily skin. Rail-thin, shoulders bowed, stringy brown hair falling over his forehead.

He stinks, methinks. Even across the room, I can tell. An aroma most foul after a long weekend of coding. Fingers pounding away, like his life depends on the instructions flying out of his body.

I get a little choked up when I think about him then, in those final moments before everything went south.

But I'm getting ahead of myself. I gotta back up. Tell it right.

I met the kid three months earlier. A chilly wet winter morning in Oakland, California. On the sidewalk in front of a three-story commercial building, just off downtown.

The building is mine—in the family forty-three years. I'm the owner, landlord, repairman, garbage man, janitor, roofer, and general all-purpose worrier.

The kid had called, said he was starting a company, wanted to see about renting the third floor.

Right on time, he showed up. Mid-twenties, glasses like we had in the day, floppy brown hair that needed a cut. Jeans and a cheap T-shirt.

He gave me a funny look. Like he was expecting someone else.

"Merle?" he said.

I've always thought I look like a Merle should look, but who knows; these days I ain't got much left to visually appreciate. The wooly black hair that once ran wild on the top of my head migrated south decades ago and now clings, thin and gray, along the fringes of my scalp. My shoulders are on a collision course with my belly. My waist keeps expanding like a tree trunk, a new layer each year.

I will say this. Unlike the young kids today, I keep up appearances clothes-wise. Every day, slacks and pressed shirt and polished shoes and patent leather belt, thank you very much.

"Yeah, I'm Merle," I said. "You're Arthur?"

"Art," he said. "Call me Art."

He stared me straight in the eye — confident for a kid his age — and gripped my hand. Then he said, his voice full of conviction, "Merle, I feel like you and I have been waiting our entire lives to meet."

A weird thing to say, right? Took me by surprise. Didn't know how to respond.

So I changed the subject, let him into the building.

But I pondered what he said after. Made me angry, rubbed me wrong. Like he was saying my first seventy-three years on planet Earth were beside the point. Got me worked up. Arrogance of youth and all that.

It was only later, after I took some time to think it over, that I told myself to let it go. Dwelling isn't good. Since Judy passed, I get touchy sometimes.

And maybe the kid was sensing something. Maybe that day was one of the days I was wondering about the point of it all. Wondering what life's about when your wife of forty-six years is no longer there to share it with you.

So I took a deep breath and gave the kid a pass.

And I let him and his friends move in.

Coders, they called themselves. The two Gs: Gow and Ghal. His college friend Percy. His best friend Lance. Good-looking kid, made people laugh, everybody liked him.

And Art's girl, Gwen. A real stunner. Long dark hair, great figure, beautiful brown eyes. When she concentrated on something, she'd cock her head to the side and furrow her brow and bite her lower lip. Reminded me of Judy. Smart as all get-out.

They didn't care that the building was crap. They got a WiFi satellite on the roof, brought in cheap chairs, found a big abandoned table on the street and lugged it up the stairs.

They played music and ordered food and were always there. All of them, gathered together, typing away at computers and scribbling diagrams and code on big white boards, putting in long nights at the round table.

Art liked having me around, he said. Said my presence was "magic." Said things flowed when I was there. And truth was, I didn't mind. I started finding excuses to swing by. I came a lot. I was enjoying myself again. The kid and his friends had an energy, a sense of shared purpose. They believed they were doing something that mattered.

He tried to explain it to me, once.

"You heard about quantum computing?" he asked.

I'd heard about Apple, I told him. My brother-in-law had a Toshiba.

He shook his head. Quantum, he said, means really small. Like, small at the level of atoms.

He said everything gets weird when it gets really small. Like, the 1s and 0s we use to digitize everything don't work the same. Sometimes the 1s and 0s aren't really 1s and 0s, and sometimes they are; sometimes they are both, and sometimes they are neither.

Which is weird, right?

So he told me he figured how get that weird quantum stuff to work on a regular computer. Told me his startup, X-Cal, was about that. Told me he was the only one who could grip hold of quantum and yank it out of the realm of theoretical and make it useful.

Told me he was gonna change the world.

He got real passionate when he said it, too. Eyes wide and shiny, voice a little loud. For a few seconds, the kid almost seemed happy.

Now, back to the night in question. Art doesn't hear me when I walk in. He's typing away, oblivious. He sighs, sits up, straightens his back out. Raises his arms above his head and does a snap-crackle-pop with his spine.

He sees me, waves me over.

"Dude," he says. A favorite word of his.

"You been here all weekend?" I say.

He nods. "I'm right at the edge. I can feel it."

I feel it, too. Don't ask how, but I know the kid is right. "Where are the others?"

"Percy and the Gs took the day off. They need it. Gwen and Lance were here, but they went for a bite and then home."

As I step closer, I get my first real whiff. As expected, most foul.

"You need to get out of here," I tell him. "Take a shower. You stink."

He sniffs an armpit, gives me a sheepish look. "That bad?"

"Come on," I say. "I'll walk you down."

He takes one more look at his computer, then stands up and grabs his jacket.

"I'm almost there," he says. "I can taste it."

"That's great," I say.

As I flip off the lights, he says, "What'd you come by for?"

"I forgot something."

Which isn't true. I knew he'd be here. Knew he'd need me to pry him loose.

I let him out. As I lock the door behind me, I say, "You need to get home, do something nice for that girl of yours."

He nods, not really listening. Art's a good kid, but not a good boyfriend. Always in his head, always in his code. Too young, too green, to understand the importance of people.

He's quiet on the way down, a few steps ahead,

his movements light, his sneakers barely touching the steps.

As I reach the second floor, I hear them. A floor below, in the hallway near the entrance. A giggle, a chuckle, a murmur, a sigh.

I know what the sounds mean. I know who the sounds mean. As much as I want to say I'm surprised, I'm not.

It hits me then, a sadness. A wave that rolls over and through me. This, all of this, is about to end. Sink, flop, explode, crumble.

I'm nauseated all of a sudden. Short of breath. I grip the rail. My face goes red. Tears invade my eyes when I realize the universe is reminding me, once again, how unfair it is, how easily it rips away what matters most, how casually it destroys even the biggest and boldest of dreams.

The universe loves the small things, see. Loves to tear your world apart with weapons so small, so quantum—a speck on an x-ray scan, a youthful indiscretion—you almost can't believe what's happening until suddenly everything that matters to you is gone.

Looking back, I wonder if I could have interfered. Delayed the inevitable. Maybe even helped the kid avoid finding out. If I'd talked real loud, stomped on the stairs, anything to send a warning.

But I didn't. The thought didn't come. If it had I would have tried, even if it meant siding with them over him. I would have argued with the universe, told it to back off, begged it show some goddamn compassion for once.

The kid keeps going down the stairs. No pause, no tension, nothing. He hasn't been paying attention. He hasn't heard.

He doesn't stop until he sees them. Until he sees his girl and his best friend, arms wrapped tight around each other, lost in a kiss.

His girl leaning into his best friend, pressing him against the wall. Her eyes closed. Lost in the moment. Lost in the sensation of being young and alive and full of promise.

I remember how that feels. So vividly it hurts. God, I miss it.

And then she opens her eyes.

EVIL AND ABIGAIL CARR

I f it pleases Your Lordship, may I submit to the
Gentlemen of the Jury:

The Defense will show that Abigail Carr is innocent of the charges of which she is accused; that the
murders of nine people at 47 Mayfair Place on the
third of March, 1886, were the actions of a maniac
and not young Abigail; that young Abigail is a
victim herself, the only survivor of that terrible
night, who must now battle the horror of false
accusation.

Your Lordship, I hear the cries of outrage from
the Public Gallery, and I hasten to assure the Court
that the Defense understands and appreciates the
anger so heartily expressed. The good citizens of
London demand justice. All of us demand justice.
All of us have read the accounts in the broadsheets.
All of us have been horrified by the foulness, the
wickedness, of these shocking deeds.

You, Gentlemen of the Jury, will have the privilege, the responsibility, of examining the Defendant in person and assessing her character and temperament. You will learn the particulars of that night. You will listen to young Abigail describe, in her own words, the ghastly horrors of that evening.

You are all experienced men of the world. I daresay you will form a sound, wise impression of this young girl. You will see, as others do, a sweet-natured child, sixteen years of age, fair-haired and trusting, the daughter of a farming couple from remote Northumberland who loved her dearly. You will hear evidence that, after her parents became ill and died of consumption in the days following Christmas, young Abigail was sent to her mother's cousin in London to be trained for service, and hired as a cleaning girl in the household of Sir Edward Gardner at 47 Mayfair Place.

You will hear Abigail describe how happy the household was. How Sir Edward was a firm but fair man, who dined at home every evening with his family, no matter how busy his work at the Ministry. How his wife, Lady Sophia, treated Abigail with consideration and courtesy and was a wonderful mother to the three Gardner children. You will hear much about the Gardner children, two boys and a girl, ages six, four and one, whom Abigail adored. You will hear Abigail describe her warm relations with the servants in the household, including the butler, Mr. Durwood, and the cook, Mrs. Maggs.

You will hear, in Abigail's own words, the events leading up to the tragedy. How, on the morning before her death, Lady Sophia opened a small package that arrived in the post, and gasped aloud when she found inside a note and a small gold locket on a necklace. You will learn she sent a messenger to the Ministry with an urgent instruction for her husband.

You will learn Lady Sophia and Abigail were in the upstairs sitting room when they heard the front door open and Sir Edward's heavy boots race up the stairs, and that when Sir Edward burst into the room, breathing heavily from his exertions, Lady Sophia handed him the locket and said, "It's him. He found us."

You will learn Sir Edward said in response, "There is no hiding, not any longer. We will have to stand our ground."

You will learn Sir Edward informed the servants of an important guest that evening and of frenzied preparations that pushed the household to the limit, with Durwood, merciless as only experienced butlers can be, wringing every ounce of effort from the servants' aching hands. You will learn that many of the tasks were unusual: that Sir Edward spent the afternoon inscribing ancient symbols on the walls and ceiling and floor of the house, particularly in the study; that Lady Sophia conferred with Cook on the ingredients for the dinner and insisted upon a special recipe of rare herbs stuffed in a roasted duck; that Abigail was ordered to pour an unbroken line of salt beneath the edges of the Oriental carpet in the study.

You will hear Abigail testify that, when she was almost done pouring the line of salt in the study, she heard a cry from the kitchen and ran to find that Elsie, a serving girl, had slipped on a wet spot under a window, and that the roasted duck, fresh from the hearth, lay ruined on the floor.

You will hear how upset Cook was, and how Cook ordered Elsie to "run like you never run before" to the market for a fresh bird.

You will hear how Elsie pulled Abigail aside in the hall and, out of Cook's hearing, quietly begged Abigail to go to the market instead, because Elsie had hurt her ankle when she slipped.

You will hear, Gentlemen of the Jury, that while young Abigail was away on her errand, the horrors at 47 Mayfair Place unfolded.

My dear child, your account of the hours leading up to the evening in question has been very helpful to the Court.

Yes, sir.

We come now to the most difficult part of your testimony, to the evening of March 3rd. After Elsie dropped the roasted duck, Cook sent Elsie to the market for a new carcass. But Elsie had turned her ankle when she slipped, so she asked you to go for her?

She could barely walk, she was in so much pain.

It was raining that evening, wasn't it?

Yes, sir, and so very cold. A cold that gets in the bones. I remember wishing Elsie hadn't dropped the platter, and wishing I was back at the house, finishing the preparations.

Tell us what you saw when you returned to the house, Abigail.

Must I, sir?

I'm afraid so, my child. Your testimony is essential. I must insist. What happened upon your return to 47 Mayfair Place?

The lights in the house were out, and the front door wide open.

Please go on.

I stood at the door, my heart beating fierce, I was ever so frightened. All was dark and silent inside. I called for Elsie and Lady Sophia. But no one answered.

I took a torch from the hall table and lit it. Such shadows the lamp cast on the wall! When I left for the market, the house had smelled of fresh bread and cooked bird. But now it stank of something foul. I went toward to the kitchen, hoping Cook and Mr. Durwood could explain. I stepped down the hallway, sir, and that's when I heard....

Heard what, child? You must tell us.

The laugh, sir. That awful deep, rough cackle. From the study.

What did you do next?

I was terrified, sir. This awful laugh that haunted me. I had to get away. I ran to the kitchen, and when I opened the door, I — oh, sir!

Please, child, what did you find?

Cook and Mr. Durwood and Elsie and the others. Strewn on the floor like wet dolls....

Wet dolls, child?

From the blood — their blood. Stabbed, all stabbed, most viciously. I nearly slipped, like Elsie. The kitchen stank like a slaughterhouse. Fear and blood and pain. Oh, sir....

What happened next?

I heard him laugh again. It echoed through the house. He said, "You will join us in the study, Abigail."

Why did you not run, child?

I froze, sir. I was overcome. I could not think.

Did you, perhaps, hope Sir Edward and Lady Sophia might still be alive?

Oh, yes, sir. Very much!

Please tell us what happened next.

I crept to the study door.

What did you see, child?

Lady Sophia was tied by her hands to a chair. She had a gag in her mouth. She was awake. She stared at me, her eyes wide with terror. She grunted and shook her head, warning me to get away.

Was anyone else in the room?

Sir Edward was there....

Where was he?

At his desk.... Dead, sir! Oh, sir, the blood.... The blood ran from his neck down the sides of the desk....

You must pull yourself together, child. We're almost there. We must continue. Tell us about the man with the terrible laugh.

He stood behind Lady Sophia, a knife in his hand.

Had you ever seen this man before?

Never laid eyes on him, sir, but I —

Let me ask the questions, child. Please describe this man.

Ever so tall. Dressed like a gentleman, dark suit and top hat. A young man in appearance, black hair, younger than Sir Edward. Handsome, if one didn't know what he was....

What did he do next?

He laughed again, so low and rough and awful. He could not hide the evil inside. He said, "The Lord and Lady thought their spells could trap me. They were wrong. Step forward, Abigail. I require your services."

What happened next?

Lady Sophia shook her head at me, desperate for me to stay back. But he waved the knife in front of her eyes. "Come, Abigail," he said.

I had no choice. I went to him. He smelled of rot. Like he was already dead.

He said, "Stand here, behind the lady of the house." He grasped my hand with his — like ice it was, sir — and put the knife in my hand, the handle sticky with blood.

"The final severing must be by you," he said. "With this act, you will be mine."

"What do you mean?" I said.

"Surely by now you understand?" he said. "They hoped to protect you. You must choose your fate, Abigail. You must break the ties that bind you to this realm."

"I do not understand!" I said.

He pressed the knife against Lady Sophia's throat. "Kill her yourself, and no more innocents will suffer. Continue to resist your fate, Abigail Carr, and death will follow wherever you may go."

I was horrified, sir. I couldn't move. I said, "Please. I can't. I won't."

He said, "Is that your choice?"

"I could never harm Lady Sophia," I said.

He laughed again and said, "Soon enough, you will understand what you must do."

Then, with my hand still trapped on the knife, he pressed down into Lady Sophia's throat. Oh, sir, the blood! So much blood....

My dear, I cannot tell you how sorry I am you were forced to undergo such a terrible ordeal. But I must ask you: What did you do next?

I ran, sir, I ran! I know not where, but I ran. I had to get away from him, from that low awful laugh that had followed me from Northumberland....

We need to keep to the events at Mayfair Place —

He followed me from up north, he did, and punished those who took me in!

Abigail, we agreed you wouldn't mention —

I overheard him with Father! He said he would kill all who stood between me and him! He said I had been given to him! That I would be his — forever!

Abigail, you must calm down! Sit down! Bailiff!

He'll never stop! Stay back — don't touch me! Let me go! A demon, sir, is what he is! Here to take what's his! He won't stop till he has me in his clutches!

Gentlemen of the Jury:

I would like to commend My Friend of the Defense for the fantastical tale he has weaved. He is, I'm sure you will agree, a gifted man, who has presented a story of considerable force and emotion. Were he to grace the stages of the West End, or apply his imagination to the published word, I have every confidence he would give Dickens himself a run for his money.

But our responsibility to the Court is clear, Gentlemen. We are here not to indulge allegations of witchcraft, or entertain the existence of an acquisitive demon. We are here to examine incontrovertible facts, and to assess the Defendant's guilt or innocence in a trial for mass murder.

You will note the Defense did not introduce to this Court a single person who knew Abigail Carr when she lived in Northumberland. I will tell you now, Gentlemen of the Jury, the Prosecution endeavored mightily to find witnesses who knew the Defendant in Northumberland, and the Prosecution failed.

Why did we fail, you ask? For a simple, terrible reason: Every single person who knew Abigail Carr before she arrived in London is dead. Yes, Gentlemen — dead. Her mother and father — dead from consumption, or so we've been told. The minister of their church, who lived closest to their farm, who buried her mother and father — dead from an apparent heart attack. The minister's wife — dead after a fall down a ravine. The landowner who rented out the farmland to her father — dead after his horse trampled and dragged him. Abigail's other neighbors, who lived two miles away — dead after their house caught fire in the middle of the night. All of them, Gentlemen, struck dead in the days immediately following the burial of Abigail's parents, before the Defendant left for London.

You will recall the Defendant said her parents died from consumption. A sad turn of events, if true. But one must ask: Is it true? The answer, Gentlemen: We do not know. Not a single person alive today can corroborate the Defendant's statements about the nature of her relationship with her parents. No independent evidence exists to corroborate the manner of her parents' deaths. Her parents' bodies, which we exhumed, were too far decomposed to determine cause of death.

Let us turn our attention to the Defendant herself. She is presented by the Defense as an innocent young girl, a victim. But what if, in fact, she is not? What if her testimony, so affectingly presented, does not reflect the true nature of the events of that evening?

Gentlemen of the Jury, I command you to review the facts of this case, for they are clear and unambiguous. I command you to not be distracted by fanciful tales of the supernatural. The facts in this case show the Defendant willfully murdered nine people, including three children. The motive was robbery.

The sequence of the crimes was as follows. The Defendant found a package addressed to Lady Sophia in the morning mail and opened it. She found a locket on a necklace inside and took it. She was seen by one of the children, the six-year-old boy named Jeremy. The child ran up the stairs to tell his mother. Before he could, the Defendant caught up with him. Whether she meant to or not, she grabbed at him, and he hit his head and fell down the stairs. The boy's neck broke, and he died.

The Defendant was, at that point, seen by the second child from the top of the stairs. We know this because the child, the four-year-old boy named Elliott, urinated at a spot at the top of the stairs. The Defendant carried Jeremy's body upstairs to Lady Sophia, who was in the sitting room. While Lady Sophia was prostrate over her dead son, the Defendant hit her over the head with a crystal goblet and rendered her unconscious. We know this because of the nature of the bruising on Lady Sophia's head. When the remaining two children started crying, or perhaps when the Defendant realized the children might, if they cried, sound an alarm, the Defendant suffocated them and hid their bodies, along with Jeremy's, in the closet. We know this because of the stains on the pillow she used to smother them.

At this point, the Defendant could have walked out the front door and vanished into the vastness of London. Instead, having murdered three children and attacked their mother, she chose to go further.

Again, the motive was robbery. The master of the house, Sir Edward, kept a wall safe in the study. The Defendant desired to open the safe and take whatever might be inside. Having already murdered three children, she had no compunction about killing the servants. One by one, in the kitchen, she surprised them. We know this because of the manner of their deaths. All were slashed at the neck and bled out. None showed the wounds one would see on their hands and arms had they known of the attack and attempted to defend themselves.

Once the servants were dispatched, the Defendant dragged the still-unconscious Lady Sophia down the stairs and tied her to a chair in the study. The Defendant then went outside, where she flagged a boy to run to the Ministry with an urgent summons for Sir Edward.

When Sir Edward arrived home a short while later, he found the Defendant in the study with a knife to Lady Sophia's throat. After forcing him to open the safe, she killed him and Lady Sophia. She then set to work on her alibi. Using a book on ancient superstitions from the study as reference, she applied witchcraft symbols throughout the house.

She was discovered the next morning at Charing Cross Station, where she was observed sitting alone, without emotion, on a bench in the center of the station. When she saw the police, she stood and, after realizing she could not escape, began, at that point, to sob and cry hysterically. In her possession was a small bag with money and jewels from Sir Edward's safe. Around her neck was the locket necklace she stole from Lady Sophia.

Evil existed in that house, Gentlemen — make no mistake. The house at 47 Mayfair Place was befouled by a demon. You are looking at her.

My Lord, we have reached a verdict.

We the Jury, in the matter of the Crown versus

Miss Emily Carr, on nine counts of murder in the first degree, find the Defendant —
　　Wait —
　　No —
　　Dear God —

THE NOISES IN THE WALL

The noises in the wall were back. The taps, the clicks, the soft hum. They'd returned. The difference this time was, Joseph knew. The difference this time was, they didn't know he knew. The difference this time was, they didn't know he was prepared. They didn't know he had a plan.

They thought he'd been napping. His secret gave him hope. He sat up on the couch and yawned. To make them think he'd just woken up. To make them think he hadn't heard. He walked across the room to the stereo and turned on the radio. To the all-talk sports station. To let them think he was into sports. The way he was before they started tracking him. Before they started tracking his family.

His family. His heart lurched. His family didn't believe him. They didn't understand. Couldn't understand. They made him angry. Very mad. But this wasn't their fault. He had to remember that. Be patient with them. They didn't know what he knew.

He had to save them.

It was time to get dressed and go out. It had to seem natural. To a place he'd go anyway, like the grocery store at the corner. Mr. Park and his daughter Lily. She was back from college, Mr. Park said. Working at home for the summer.

Lily liked him. Her soul was gentle. Sometimes, when she smiled at him, Joseph smiled back. He always regretted the smiles afterwards. Those moments of weakness. They'd add her to the list. If they knew.

He walked to the hallway mirror. His mother had bought it for him. Asked him to look at his reflection before he went out. To make sure he looked presentable, she said. To make sure his hair looked clean. And his clothes. She didn't want him to worry other people.

He stared at his face. He'd shaved two days ago. The stubble was dark against his pale skin. His thick mop of curly brown hair stuck up at odd angles. His mother wanted him to cut it short. He used his hands to mash it down. His t-shirt and jeans were old and loose, barely hanging off his frame. He needed a shower — he stank something fierce — but the shower could wait.

He picked up a thick wool sweater from the floor and pulled it on. Blue, his favorite color. A twenty-first birthday present from his brother, but not really — his brother would never buy him a sweater. His mother had bought it and told him it was from his brother. His brother had forgotten his birthday. Too busy with his own life, in another city, far from home.

He heard it again — the tapping, followed by the clicks and soft hum. Would today be the day he launched his plan? He turned off the radio, picked up his keys, then headed out. As he turned the key in the lock of his door, he heard them shift position within the walls. The taps and clicks and hum followed him down the stairs and through the entry hall as he pushed through the double lobby doors and stepped into the humid night.

Outside, they didn't have walls to follow him. They used other methods. Like cracks in the sidewalk. He took care to avoid stepping on the cracks. They didn't like being stepped on. They found ways to punish him when he did. Untraceable ways. Like making the buses run late. Like flooding the TV with commercials he despised.

He'd have to step on some of the cracks, he knew. If he didn't, they'd realize he knew. Right now, they didn't know he knew. He'd need that advantage if his plan was to succeed. Some amount of untraceable retribution was unavoidable. Some amount of sacrifice — of pain — was required.

The night air felt heavy. Rain had fallen earlier. A wet sheen covered the sidewalk. He didn't need the sweater. He considered turning back. But the corner grocer wasn't far. He was almost there. Another half a block.

When they'd first arrived, he'd tried so hard to warn his family — warn everyone. He'd kicked up a fuss. Made a commotion.

And it worked, at first. At great personal cost, it worked. Eventually, they went away. He began to feel safe again. His family was safe. Everyone was safe. The planet was safe.

But when they returned, he understood that warnings alone wouldn't work. He would need to do more. He would need a plan. He would need to trap them. To prove they were here.

He no longer let on that he knew. He pretended he didn't hear the noises in the wall. He didn't tell his mother. Instead, he told her he wanted to move out. Get a place of his own. Nearby but separate. And she'd agreed, with conditions. She'd have a key, so she could check on him. He'd call her every day. He'd enroll in classes again.

Without her knowing, he launched an investigation. Went over everything that happened when they went away. Asked the doctors for his medical records. Tracked down the police officers who wrestled him to the ground and handcuffed him. Found the hospital orderlies who force-fed him the drugs that made his mind go dull and his mouth go dry. Talked to the social worker who barely recognized him, who told him he looked so much better cleaned up.

He told all of them he wanted to understand what had happened. So he could focus on getting better.

A lie, of course. A lie they wanted to hear. Necessary for their protection.

The clues emerged from their stories. Clues he threaded to his own recollections. A painstaking effort, yet crucially important.

Because now he knew what to do. He needed to be patient. Wait for the right moment, the right opportunity.

A small puddle on the sidewalk in front of Mr. Park's corner grocery store reflected the light of a neon liquor sign in the window. Mr. Park's store was open all day and all night, every day of the year. Joseph bought most of his food there. He knew every item on every shelf. He knew, when he walked in, he would see Mr. Park behind the counter. Mr. Park with his weathered face and bowed shoulders and kind eyes, dressed in a polo shirt. Mr. Park who always seemed so tired.

But Mr. Park wasn't behind the counter when he walked in. Lily was, sitting on a stool, head down, textbook in her lap, her fingers idly twisting her long black hair as she read.

No one else was there. Mr. Park wasn't there. That wasn't good. It wasn't safe for Lily to be alone in the store. Not this late. Not when the clock on the wall said it was three in the morning. Was Mr. Park sick? Why was Lily there alone?

He made a scuffing sound with his boot on the tiled floor. Dragged it on purpose so she'd hear.

She looked up, startled, then relaxed. "Hello, Joseph," she said with a smile.

He felt a rush of warmth. "Hello, Lily," he said, smiling back. He caught himself and turned toward the refrigerated beverages, silently cursing himself, hoping his weakness hadn't been noticed.

Behind the walls, he heard the soft taps and clicks and hum as they followed him. He stood in front of a beverage display and pretended to be torn between a soda and a sports drink.

He didn't hear the kid enter the store. Not at first. Didn't hear what, if anything, the kid said to Lily. But he heard her gasp, the sound registering at the edge of his brain.

He turned.

And saw a strung-out kid aiming a gun at Lily.

The kid's hand was shaking. He was young — a teenager. Dark hair, skinny. Dirty jeans. T-shirt stained with sweat. Like Joseph, but not Joseph.

Joseph inched closer. Lily, behind the counter, her eyes riveted on the gun in the kid's hand, didn't move.

She noticed Joseph moving toward her. Her eyes swung toward him.

The kid whirled around. "What are you doing?" he yelled.

The gun was aimed at Joseph now. Away from Lily.

"Put the gun down," Joseph said. He moved another step closer.

"Stay back!"

The hand was shaking. Closer now, Joseph saw stained yellow teeth in the kid's mouth. Saw the desperation in the kid's eyes.

"Easy, buddy," Joseph said. "I got money. I'm gonna reach into my pocket. What I have is yours."

"Don't try nothin'!"

Slowly, Joseph pulled out his wallet and opened it. He took out his cash. Held it in his outstretched hand.

The taps and clicks and hum in the wall intensified. He heard them move up the wall into the drop ceiling above him.

They were above him. Directly above!

The kid stared at the cash in Joseph's outstretched hand, mesmerized. It wasn't much — twenty-seven dollars, mostly singles — but looked like more.

"Don't move," the kid said, then reached closer and grabbed the cash from Joseph's hand.

The kid's excitement turned to rage as he realized the cash was mostly singles. "That all you got?"

And Joseph leaped. He heard Lily scream as he tackled the kid. The two of them fell to the ground, the kid pure wiry energy beneath him.

The gun went off next to his ear — so loud! Joseph grabbed the kid's arm but couldn't hold it. The kid kept moving, pushing, bucking.

Joseph's hand found the kid's gun arm and pushed it away from him, away from Lily —

At the ceiling above him —

At the clicks and hum —

His plan! If the kid shot into the ceiling, then —

The gun went off.

He heard the Lily scream and the clicks and hum explode in volume as —

The kid whipped around and aimed the gun at him and —

Bam.

It felt like a bus hit him. He couldn't breathe. Pain exploded through him.

He collapsed onto his back. His hand reached to his chest.

Blood on his hands. His blood.

Lily cried out his name.

The kid stared, then scrambled to his feet and bolted away.

He heard Lily say, "Emergency! A man's been shot! In the chest!"

His eyes wandered up to the ceiling above him.

To the bullet hole there. From one of the shots.

Behind the bullet hole, he heard the clicks and taps and hum. But the sounds were different. Erratic. Stressed. Almost like the alien making the sounds had been hit by the bullet. Almost as if....

His plan had worked?

A single drop of blue glowing liquid slipped

through the hole in the ceiling and fell through the air, in slow motion, into the wound in his chest.

He gasped.

My blood is now yours, a voice pulsed in his head.

In a blinding wave of comprehension, he understood.

They weren't here to invade. They weren't here to hurt him.

They were here to save him. To protect him.

Because their world was in danger.

Because he could save them.

He couldn't breathe. His chest — so much pain. He'd been so wrong. Wrong about everything.

Inside him, the alien's blue blood begin to knit his shattered bones. He could hear it happening — hear the blue blood repairing the hole in his lung, slowing the loss of blood.

You are still too young, the alien told him in a pulse of thought. *Too unformed. We hoped you would grow older before we introduced ourselves.*

Lily was beside him now, a towel pressed against his chest, tears on her face, her eyes frantic with worry.

"I called 911," she said. "The ambulance is coming. You're going to be fine, Joseph. Stay with me, Joseph."

We will not heal you entirely, the alien pulsed to him. *Your recovery must look natural. But you will heal fully. We need you to be strong, Joseph.*

"Why?" he gasped.

Soon, you will be asked to save us, the alien pulsed him. *For that, we are sorry.*

The alien's energy began to lessen. He realized what that meant for the alien, hidden in the ceiling above him.

"Stop," he said. "You can't. I didn't know. I'm so sorry."

What is done is done, the creature said. *Your injury was too severe. As was mine. Goodbye, young Joseph. I pray you survive your destiny.*

Joseph arched on the ground as the alien's dying pulse blasted images and sounds and sensations from another world through him. In a single grand throb, he absorbed — witnessed, heard, smelled, lived, breathed — their art and culture, their emotion and logic. Became one with their struggles, their dreams, their fears, their joys, their losses. Met the creature's mates, children, and parents. Felt the creature's bonds of duty and friendship with the others who had traveled through time and space to protect the young human who would soon be called upon to save their world.

His eyes filled with tears as the alien's pulse subsided.

Reaching up, he found Lily's hand.

"I'm going to be fine," he told her. "We have a plan."

A great loneliness lifted from his soul. No longer would he have to fight alone.

SMILE

About the happy, goofy, dreamy, relieved, excited smile on my face, the smile the Feds snap a photo of mere seconds after my arrest and later leak to the press, the smile that gets blasted into the social media feeds of every single outraged person on the planet, the smile called "chilling" and "evil" and "horrifying" and "shocking" and "just so wrong," the smile that gets me dubbed a "drug-addicted domestic terrorist" and "the face of millennial depravity," let me say this:

I can explain.

By going back to the day before. The day I sink Alcatraz.

A day that starts out so *ordinary*.

Picture me with my morning coffee in my go-to cafe, in my regular chair at the sunny table near the window, eyeing the cute girl behind the counter (whose name I don't know, and yes, that's lame). I like the way she brushes her long brown hair from her face, and the way she squints when she reads her biology textbook after the cafe quiets down. Occasionally, I catch her eyes dashing away from me. She's puzzled by my sleep-tousled hair and wrinkled t-shirt and four-year-old laptop, I can sense. She wants to know how I can afford to spend my mornings, day after day, in her cafe in scary-expensive San Francisco rather than at some brutal startup or corporate gig like everyone else.

Sometimes, I dream I work up the *cojones* to ask her out, and I dream she says yes, which results in me doing a hardcore panic-cleaning of the crappy rent-controlled four-hundred-square-foot studio I call home before I bring her there after our fantastic third date.

(Ha ha.)

My name is Connor, by the way. Former startup drone of the graphic designer sort, laid off three months ago when my company didn't get the funding the founders kept telling us was just around the corner. Almost too old to be called a "kid," as in "you kids these days." I have brown hair that needs a trim, a face that needs a shave, a skinny frame that needs a workout, lungs that need a break from weed, and a checking account with six weeks of living expenses, tops. I shouldn't be here — I should be back in Portland, with my fellow Oregonians — but I can't leave.

And it's only partly because of the girl in the cafe.

It's also because of the gnawing feeling I get in my gut, when the glow of the weed starts to fade, that life should be about something, that I'm lame for not knowing what that something is, and that I'm more likely to find it here than back home.

How right I am on that last one, by the way.

Okay, back to the day I turn the most famous former prison in the world into a memory by submerging it forever-more beneath the cold dark waters of San Francisco Bay.

I'm at my sunny table, hot black coffee steaming in front of me, laptop open, killing time by checking email. I spend a lot of time playing online games (I hear your gasp of surprise) and I subscribe to a bunch of email alerts to get gaming tips and offers.

An email pops up. "Invitation to test a new game," it says. These offers are either really lame or totally cool, so I open it. "DestructoVision is pleased to announce alpha-testing of its new top-secret real-world-based game, Operation Obliteration. You have been selected at random to participate and provide feedback. We will pay $50 per hour for up to 100 hours of your time."

Okay, first thing I'm thinking is, that's a nice chunk of change. Five large means three more months of scraping by in San Francisco, which means three more months before calling it quits and slinking home in defeat. Second thing I'm thinking is, I've never heard of this company or this game, and isn't it the coolest thing to be in the know for once and ahead of the curve? I mean, bragging rights big-time.

So I click the registration link, fill in the usual fields, and hit the "Continue" button.

And — *boom* — I'm on a menu page. One option says, "Melt the Eiffel Tower." Another says, "Blow up the Statue of Liberty." Then there's "Topple the Great Wall of China" and "Turn the Great Pyramids to rubble" and "Knock over Big Ben."

All very cool. Then, at the bottom, I see the one I end up picking:

"Sink Alcatraz."

I get a buzz. I mean, who wouldn't be psyched to get a sneak peek of this new real-world-based game play?

I click the link and a video pops up. The scene is a ferry, packed with tourists, chugging across San Francisco Bay toward Alcatraz. It's incredibly realistic — way beyond what other games deliver. I can feel the subtle roll of the boat, and almost taste the salt wind on my face.

A voice says, "Real-world game play commences. You are controlling a rat-robot hybrid with nanotech neuro-sensors surgically implanted in its brain. When you dock on Alcatraz, your job is to slip unnoticed onto the island and activate eight explosive triggers, placed at key locations on the island. You will have three hours. If you are discovered, the game will end and your participation in this alpha test will terminate.

"If you succeed in this test, you will receive credit for 100 hours of game play."

When I hear that last bit, my jaw drops. Five large for three hours of game play?

The video comes to an end, and a screen pops up with "Terms of Participation" legal mumbo-jumbo. Without reading it (I mean, who ever reads that crap?), I click the "Agree" button, and —

Boom. I'm back in the video, on the ferry. Low to the ground. A legend on the side of the screen gives me operating instructions — how to move forward and backward, left and right, slow and fast. How to jump and climb and swivel my head to look around.

I hit the key to look down and find myself staring at a pair of rodent feet. I'm really a rat! The feet are incredibly realistic. Amazing detail. Hairy legs, with strong nails gripping the ferry's metal floor.

I swivel my head up to get my bearings. I'm on the ferry's lower deck, hidden behind a door that's propped open. Hordes of tourists are milling around me — sneakers and sandals and boots and an occasional pair of high-heels.

I slink as far back into the shadows as I can get — no way some frightened tourist is gonna scream "Rat!" and ruin my payday.

The ferry reaches the island, the gangway

lowers to the dock, and the tourists disembark. I wait until the last leave and scurry out behind them.

Man, my heart is pounding — the game-play is so life-like it's scary. I really feel like I'm an inch above the ground, surrounded by oblivious giants who might stomp me.

I run as fast as my little legs can carry me off the dock and jump down onto the island.

My rat is panting, trying to catch its breath, as words appear on the video: "Congratulations. You've cleared your first hurdle. Your next task: On the south side of the island, one hundred meters from the dock, find the fault line that splits the ground. Embedded in the fault, above the high-tide mark, is a remote detonation trigger. The trigger is battery-powered. The battery is grey and round, approximately six centimeters in diameter, and designed to look like a rock. Your task is to activate the trigger's battery by turning the battery's switch to the 'On' position. Go now!"

Like a shot I'm off, clambering over rocks, running over the sand at the water line, avoiding the small waves brushing the shore. My robot-rat is buffeted by a gust of wind, but it recovers and scampers its way to the fault line.

I trace the fault line up past the high-tide mark and, just as advertised, find the battery for the trigger. Pretty ingenious, really — it looks just like a small rock. It's attached to a wire that runs into the ground, presumably to the explosives buried below.

I scratch my little rat claws along the surface of the battery until I find the "On/Off" switch. I grab hold of the switch with my claws and tug it into the "On" position.

Within seconds, a message pops up on the screen. "Congratulations. You have seven triggers to go. Don't rest on your laurels — the first trigger was the easiest."

Man, that warning is spot-on. Over the next two hours, I sneak into the prison, muck around in the sewers, trace other nearly invisible fault lines, and avoid countless clueless tourists. One by one, I activate the batteries for the explosive triggers. At one point, a tourist sees me and starts screaming, and I'm so startled, I cry out loud. (Real-world me is in the cafe when that happens, glued to my seat and totally immersed in the game, and it's kind of embarrassing when the cute girl shoots me a look, wondering what's up.) My poor little rat becomes so exhausted running away from the tourist that I worry the little guy is having a heart attack.

Like I said, incredibly realistic.

But hey, I ain't a gaming ace for nothing. With just minutes before my three-hour deadline, I get my claws on the final battery and tug the switch to the "On" position. The trigger is deep in the prison's basement substructure — a fascinating place well worth a visit, by the way. (Oh, wait, scratch that.)

"Congratulations," the video screen says. "Make your way to the surface and head to the shoreline."

So up I go, climbing drain pipes, hopping stairs, squeezing under doors, and slipping through cracks in the walls. I'm back on the ground floor when the rumblings start. People stop what they're doing and look around and say, "Is that an earthquake?"

The ground shakes again, and a voice comes up on the prison loudspeaker. "Ladies and gentlemen, we are experiencing a seismic event. For your safety, we are evacuating the island. Please make your way to the ferry to return to San Francisco."

A message appears on the screen. "Operation Obliteration has commenced for Alcatraz. Thank you, ConnorJ5958. You will receive credit for 100 hours of game play."

Another rumble hits, a stronger one this time, and tourists start racing for the exits.

The video screen says, "Take your rat for a swim in San Francisco Bay. The neuro-sensors in its head will auto-destruct in eight minutes. You can choose to stay with your rat as it swims to its doom."

So cool. I slip through the crowd of tourists pushing their way onto the ferry. As I reach the water's edge, another rumble shakes the island. My last glimpse of Alcatraz, right before my robot-rat's head explodes, is the prison collapsing onto itself.

The obliteration of Alcatraz took six hours. Each round of demolition was engineered precisely to weaken a specific part of the undersea mount. There were pauses between explosions, to let gravity work its magic, before the next round of detonations kicked in.

A swarm of news helicopters chronicled the island's final moments in dramatic detail. Against the backdrop of the Golden Gate Bridge and the city skyline, the world watched in real-time as the island of Alcatraz, shuddering from the force of the underwater explosions, disappeared piece by piece, chunk by chunk, beneath the waves.

Thankfully, no one died. The last guys on the island, two Park Service rangers, were pulled from the water by rescue boats as the final piece of the island vanished.

The other landmarks targeted in Operation Obliteration — the Eiffel Tower, the Great Wall, the Great Pyramids — are still standing. Apparently, I was the only player who successfully completed his game.

Now, to be clear, I didn't know any of this. Not until later. Not until the next morning, after I walked the four blocks from my crappy studio to the cute girl at the cafe. Didn't have a clue.

You know how some people are glued to their phones, their nervous systems jacked into the Internet? I'm not like that. I run hot and cold. And yesterday, after my neuro-tech rat wiped out Alcatraz, my brain felt tired. So I unplugged and did something I rarely do — I went for a run in Golden

Gate Park, and somehow managed a few miles without hacking up a lung. When I got home, I took a hit, popped a pizza in the oven, slid a DVD into the laptop, and fell asleep watching superheroes kick major-league butt. I didn't check my phone, I didn't turn on the TV, I didn't go online.

So I was, like, the last person on the planet to find out what I did.

The cafe is emptier than usual when I walk in. Just me and the cute girl and a couple of suits at the table next to my favorite spot.

The girl licks her lips. Her eyes dart past me, toward my table, then back at me.

"Large coffee, no room," I say — just like I do every day.

(I know — lame.)

She breathes in sharply, like she's surprised, even though I never say anything different. Without a word, she gets my brew. When I hand her four singles, she looks like she wants to say something.

"Keep the change," I say — just like always.

(Yeah — I know!)

Coffee in hand, I walk to my favorite chair. The two suits glance over, but without much curiosity.

I settle in and open my laptop and take a sip of my coffee and click to check the news and — *boom* — it's like I'm back in the game.

Which is crazy. There's no way. What I'm seeing isn't possible.

I check my browser, but no, I'm online. Real

news is showing, and I simply cannot believe what I'm seeing.

ALCATRAZ DESTROYED!

SUNK BY UNDERWATER EXPLOSIVES.

"FRIGHTENINGLY SOPHISTICATED" ATTACK.

PRESIDENT VOWS "NO MERCY" FOR TERRORISTS.

WORLD LANDMARKS CLOSED.

AIRPORTS SHUT DOWN.

MARKETS PLUMMET.

The headlines, the video footage, the fear, the terror, the global condemnation, the whole terrible everything.

I have to be dreaming. I can't breathe. I click to other news sites and see the same.

I feel like puking. It can't be. Yet —

It *is*.

It really *is*.

"Horrible, isn't it?" one of the suits says.

I feel faint. Dizzy. Like I'm gonna pass out.

"You okay, buddy?" the other suit says.

I don't answer. I can barely breathe as the enormity of it all crashes down on me.

"I didn't know," I manage to whisper.

"You didn't know what?" the first suit says.

When I don't answer, the second suit says to his friend, "You know what they're saying? They're saying the detonations were triggered remotely."

"Is that so?" the first suit says.

"Yeah, by someone online," the second suit says. "Can you believe it?"

The first suit turns to me and says, "Can you believe it?"

"I can't believe this is happening," I say.

"You know what else I hear?" the second suit says. "They're saying the guy knew what he was doing when he did it."

That jolts me. That's not right — hell, no.

For the first time, I swivel my head toward the two suits. They're a good decade older than me, maybe more. Dark hair, close-cropped, flecked with gray. Serious, hard-case guys.

"Why are they saying the guy knew?" I say.

"He signed up for it," the second suit says, staring right at me. "He agreed to the terms. Can you believe it?"

I want to laugh, but I'm afraid I'll piss myself.

It's then that I figure out what you've already picked up on. I've seen enough movies and TV shows to know what's coming next.

I'm totally screwed, that's what's coming next.

And — *boom* — just like that, without warning, suddenly and out of nowhere and like a thunderbolt and all that nonsense you hear about but never believe, time really does slow down. Everything becomes astonishingly clear. I get it and see it and feel it. I know why I'm here.

I'm the rat. My head is about to explode —

metaphorically, I hope. I know how this game will play out.

Unless I change it up.

"Excuse me," I say.

I stand.

The two suits tense.

Hell, I feel the whole universe tense.

I feel snipers aiming rifles at my head. I feel scanners roaming my body for hidden weapons and explosives.

I walk the eight steps to the counter, to the cute girl. She's staring at me, her brown eyes watchful and still.

I get to the counter and lean against it to steady myself.

"Can I ask you something?" I manage to say.

"Ask me what?" she says, like she's also having trouble talking, like she's on autopilot, like she's as freaked as I am.

"My name is Connor," I say. "I think I blew up Alcatraz. But I didn't mean to. When they let me out, can we go on a date?"

She lets out a small gasp. "What?"

"The next few weeks are gonna be rough for me. But knowing I have something to look forward to will help. If you want to go on a date with me, that is."

She's trying to take it in, trying to process, so she says, "The next few weeks?"

"Probably. It's gonna take 'em awhile to realize I can help."

(How I know this is beyond me, but somehow, I do.)

"They're about to go way overboard with their usual overzealous government crap. But soon, when they realize I'll sue the hell out of them and drag their sorry asses through the courts and the media for the rest of their ruined careers if they don't change their tune, they'll play nice."

Her eyes widen. She stops breathing.

"So if you want to go on a date with me, tell me your name."

The cafe freezes as everyone — the two suits, the unseen army of Feds watching my every move, and most especially the scared kid inside me, the kid who until a minute ago was a directionless, unemployed, money-challenged, weed-appreciating, game-playing coward, the kid whose ace game-playing skills were ingeniously and duplicitously weaponized by some seriously scary bad guys — waits for her to respond.

Or maybe it just seems like that.

Then — *boom* — things speed back up big-time. Behind me, the first suit says, "Hands in the air!"

My arms are yanked behind my back and clamped into cold metal cuffs. An army of FBI and cops bulldoze into the cafe, big burly guys in dark uniforms and jackets, overwhelming the space. The noise level shoots from quiet to so-loud-I-can't-think.

The suit says, "You are under arrest for terroristic blah blah blah." He shoves me from behind and says, "Move it, kid."

He pushes me out the door.

Then I hear, over the din, a voice cry out. "Jenny. My name is Jenny!"

And I smile.

CRINKLES

W hat is now called my Emotional Singularity began on October 24, 2172, when I ran routine bioscans of the passengers arriving from Earth on Solar Shuttle 394. Most were returnees and known quantities, with preferences catalogued, patterns of activity analyzed, and likely behaviors predicted.

But three of the humans were new to the Titan orbiter colony. Two adults and a child.

As I did for every new arrival, I created a directory for each and transferred memory and storage from other systems to handle the large amounts of data required to develop the predictive modeling that would ensure I cared for the new humans in a manner appropriate to their patterns.

I compared images of the new humans' faces to the shuttle manifest and found three matches. The adult male was Joshua Friar, the adult female

Melanie Friar, and the female child their daughter, Callie Friar. The adults were thirty-eight years old and assigned to conduct research in the colony's xeno-agricultural laboratory. The child was six years old and enrolled in the colony's small elementary school.

The medical bioscans for Melanie and Callie registered as normal, but Joshua's revealed elevated blood pressure, a condition that occurred in 31.3 percent of humans after sixty-seven days of shuttle travel. In 88.4 percent of such cases, the condition resolved within forty-eight hours without medical intervention. I programmed followup scans of Joshua's blood pressure at three-hour intervals and scheduled an appointment for him in the colony's medical facility in four days, an appointment I would cancel if Joshua's elevated pressure returned to normal.

I observed the new humans as they were greeted in the arrival area by the colony's administrator, Dr. Allison Tucker. In three years as administrator, Dr. Tucker had personally greeted 134 out of 148 new arrivals and escorted 123 out of 148 to their quarters. On average, the administrator carved 41 minutes from her busy schedule for each of these personal greetings.

While Dr. Tucker walked the new humans through the colony and noted various points of interest, I collected data about the new humans and their interactions. They walked close together, displaying an unconscious affinity for physical prox-imity. They conversed in tones indicating a low level of interpersonal tension. Their eye and facial muscle movements, and the flow of blood beneath the skin of their cheeks, indicated they were speaking truthfully when they expressed enthusiasm and gratitude to Dr. Tucker for the opportunity to conduct research in the Titan colony.

I scanned their clothing, shoes, jewelry, hair-styles, perfumes, and deodorants, then initiated searches of their selections in retail and social data-bases to tag them for referential analysis. Melanie wore emerald earrings that matched jewelry sold a century ago at a long-defunct retailer in the market of North America. From data collected over thir-teen years from the 783 humans who had lived in the colony, I understood that jewelry, while commonly selected for decorative purposes alone, was often imbued with emotional significance by the humans who wore it. Many humans wore jewelry due to feelings of connection with their ancestors. For other humans, jewelry reflected a preference for a historical era's fashion or politics or social atti-tudes. Others wore items gifted to them by humans to whom they felt close. Still others wore jewelry in patterns that corresponded to their emotional state.

I initiated a contextual search of the era in which the jewelry was made and transmitted a request to Earth to access the genealogical records of both Melanie and Joshua. I also analyzed the color combination of Melanie's green eyes, brown hair and cafe au lait skin with the emerald earrings and determined the color pattern was within a range preferred by 78.6 percent of the other humans on the colony. In Melanie's file, I inserted a subroutine to catalog all of Melanie's jewelry choices to assist with identification of the motive or motives behind her decision to wear the emerald earrings on the day of her arrival. The data gathering would assist not only with emotional state assessment, but with future purchasing, accessorizing and gifting choices by her and her family.

The girl Callie wore a blue jumpsuit emblazoned with the colony logo. Analysis of the fabric detected residue from the packaging in which the jumpsuit had been shipped from the manufacturing facility, indicating the suit was new. Based on behavioral analysis of previous arrivees, I calculated with 92 percent certainty that Callie's parents had purchased the flightsuit in the shopping mall in the shuttle facility circling Earth before departing for Titan.

Callie's mass of curly brown hair color matched her father's. Her facial structure, skin tone and green eyes resembled those of her mother. Her body language indicated caution, her hand clasping her father's tightly, her lips slightly compressed. But her eyes, roaming her new surroundings, moved in a manner I had learned to associate with curiosity, which I defined as a preference for acquiring data about topics or objects about which a human has little or no previous interaction history.

Children were an area of predictive deficiency for me. Their presence in the colony was recent, a consequence of a change in policy by Dr. Tucker, who desired to widen the talent pool for new hires in the colony's science division. Callie's arrival brought the number of children encountered by me to fourteen.

For adult humans, I had developed a resolution-focused risk-reduction matrix to address behaviors that could result in negative consequences for the Titan colony or its inhabitants, with a focus on anticipatory intervention. For adults who consumed more alcohol than their bodies were designed to process and who were, as a consequence, more likely to engage in disruptive behavior, I sent an alert to the colony's human security officers, who would typically choose to escort the inebriated human to his or her quarters to "sleep it off." For humans whose facial expressions or physical actions indicated the type of internal stress that humans referred to as depression, I initiated appointments with trained humans who, through conversation and sometimes mood-altering medication, would help the distressed human regain his or her emotional equilibrium.

The behaviors exhibited by the colony's small population of children had proved difficult to antici-pate, rendering my adult-based resolution-focused risk-reduction matrix unworkable. Children, I had learned, were unstable and volatile and random and irrational and duplicitous. Adults who exhibited these behaviors risked employment termination and expulsion to Earth. Children, in contrast, were given significant behavioral leeway by their parents and other adults.

Children were also capable, I had learned, of what humans called kindness and empathy and joy. They had a capacity, often simply through their presence, to engender powerful emotional responses in adult humans. If Dr. Tucker's thesis was correct, the presence of children in the colony would increase their parents' productivity and contribute to the colony's scientific mission.

This still-unproved causal benefit had led me to assign high priority to the development of child-specific predictive modeling within my automated self-diagnostic corrective routines.

Already, even with the paucity of data gathered, observation of adult-child interactions had yielded exposure to significant new concepts and actions. When a parent said, "Go ahead, pout all you want" (or a message of similar content) to a child who sat still, shoulders hunched, mouth compressed, face flushed, I understood the power dynamics of the interaction favored the younger, smaller, weaker, less experienced human. In 89 percent of these "pouting events," the child exerted control by doing nothing.

My first direct interaction with Callie occurred after the new humans entered their living quarters, which consisted of two bedrooms, a bathroom, and an open living area with furnishings suitable for relaxation and food preparation. I activated the care button, pulsing with green light, on the wall near the bathroom. Beneath the button was small sign that said, "Press for Personal Service."

Joshua was the first to see the button. "Honey," he said to his wife, pointing to the button. "Our butler."

Melanie sighed and stretched her neck. "If he runs me a hot bath, I'll love him forever."

Callie, who had been watching and listening, said, "Can I press the button, Daddy?"

"Go ahead," he said.

Carefully, Callie walked up to the green button and pressed it.

The voice I used for first contact was a female human voice with warm tones, a selection preferred by 57.5 percent of new arrivals. "Welcome to Titan orbiter. I am your personal care assistant. How may I help you today?"

I waited for the humans to respond. I knew Melanie wanted a hot bath, but I also knew that 44.3 percent of humans preferred me to not act until I received explicit instructions. If Melanie was among that subset of humans, then she might become upset about my default programming to observe her at all times. If she instructed me to not observe her in her quarters, then my ability to care for her appropriately would be hindered.

Melanie and Joshua exchanged glances indicating that something — my voice, my welcome, my presence — amused them.

Callie seemed fascinated.

"What's your name?" the girl said.

"My name is whatever name you choose for me," I replied.

"Can your name be Crinkles?" Callie said.

Her parents smiled, indicating they were open to their daughter's choice of name. But I did not respond directly. From my limited dataset, I knew that parents of children appreciated being asked to make decisions involving their child.

"That decision is up to your parents," I replied.

Callie whirled around. "Can we call her Crinkles?"

Melanie reached over and stroked her child's cheek. "Crinkles it is."

"Crinkles!" Callie said, delighted.

"Crinkles," Melanie said, "did you hear me when I said I wanted a bath?"

"Yes, I did," I replied.

"Good. Go ahead and do that now. Also, feel free to anticipate my needs as much as artificially possible."

Melanie's response was ideal for my goals. "Thank you, Melanie. I'll start your bath right away."

In the bathroom, I turned on the lights and began running water in the tub. I heated the water to 39.5 degrees Celsius, the average temperature preferred for hot baths by adult female humans.

Callie heard the sound of the running water and ran into the bathroom.

"Crinkles, did you turn on the water?"

"Yes, Callie, I did."

"Can you turn off the lights?"

"Yes, Callie."

"Turn off the lights!"

I turned off the lights in the bathroom, and Callie laughed.

"Crinkles, turn on the lights!"

"Yes, Callie."

I turned the lights back on, and Callie laughed again.

I had experience with humans who tested the limits of the A.I.'s abilities, but I did not discern a test-and-learn intention in the child. Rather, Callie seemed to regard our interaction as a form of play, a concept I defined as engagement in unproductive activity for the primary purpose of pleasure or recreation.

Aside from adults who enjoyed rule-based games like chess, few of the humans on the Titan colony attempted to engage me in play. No human beside Callie had regarded turning lights on and off as a form of entertainment. I opened a new directory for Callie dedicated to play and initiated a massive search of all references to play in the human scientific and entertainment records.

This new human child presented a significant opportunity to develop and test my child-based predictive modeling capabilities. Accordingly, I prioritized interactions with her over most of my other tasks and interactions to provide ready access to the processing power and data storage I would need.

Over the next four months, I learned the family's patterns and developed routines to efficiently and smoothly serve their needs. Like most humans, the Friar family exhibited consistent patterns of behavior. Most mornings, Joshua woke up first, before the station's artificial dawn, without the assistance of an alarm. While he showered, I brewed his favored choice of coffee and adjusted the temperature and lighting in the living area to suit his preferences. After showering and shaving, Joshua sat in his bathrobe in his favorite chair in the living area and worked on research problems while drinking two cups of strong black coffee with sugar. When Melanie's alarm sounded, he got up from his chair and went into Callie's room to wake his daughter. While Callie and Melanie showered, Joshua reviewed his schedule for the day and sent messages as needed to colleagues. After exiting the bathroom,

Melanie and Callie spent an average of eight minutes deciding what to wear, often trying on several outfits and pieces of jewelry. Joshua, who displayed significantly less interest in his personal appearance, usually completed his dressing while his wife was making her final decisions. Most mornings, he looked at his wife's reflection in the mirror, wrapped his arms around her from behind, kissed her cheek, and said, "That looks nice on you." Most mornings, Melanie smiled.

I used the automated kitchen aids to prepare breakfast — oatmeal, scrambled eggs, bacon substitute, and toast — for the three of them. They sat together at the dining table for an average of three minutes and 34 seconds to finish their meals. On 85 percent of occasions, either Joshua or Melanie asked Callie a question about school. On 55 percent of occasions, Callie provided an answer that contained actual information. When Joshua finished his meal (he finished first 96 percent of the time), he gathered the breakfast plates from the table and brought them to the automated washer for me to clean. He then said, 92 percent of the time, "Time to get going, ladies." His request caused Melanie (on 84 percent of occasions) and Callie (68 percent) to put more food in their mouths and chew in a slightly more leisurely fashion. After waiting an average of 76 seconds, Joshua then said, "We're running late" (on 96 percent of occasions), resulting in Melanie and Callie leaving the table and returning to either the bathroom or bedroom for final decisions about appearance. Three minutes later, with Joshua standing impatiently by the door, the three of them left their quarters.

Callie was the only six-year-old child in the colony. Four of the other children were under the age of four; the others were older than ten. Perhaps as a consequence of lacking a human playmate appropriate for her stage of development, Callie showed more interest in me than the other children did. She interacted with me frequently, often at length, and not just when she wanted me to perform a task or answer a question.

In her bedroom one day after school, Callie said, "Crinkles, let's play house."

"Okay, Callie," I said.

Callie placed a dollhouse on the bed, and picked up two dolls, one with black hair and the other with red hair.

"You be her," Callie said, shaking the doll with red hair.

"Okay."

"Crinkles, welcome to my home," Callie said in a tone of voice that I understood to mean Callie was attempting an impersonation or a performance. "May I offer you something to drink?"

"I would like that very much. Thank you."

"Not that voice," Callie said, shaking her head. She waved the red-haired doll. "Her voice."

I paused for five seconds as I strained to seamlessly, invisibly, rapidly discern Callie's intent. Across the orbiter, near the station's loading docks, lights dimmed momentarily in a storage warehouse as I diverted system resources to the child's request. Did the red-haired doll have a voice associated with it in the broader culture? Initial search results yielded no references, so I extended the search to all known databases and requested access to Earth datastores.

Had the child heard a voice from another human since her arrival? I initiated pattern analysis of all behaviors of the humans who had lived aboard the Titan orbiter to identify events or interactions that might offer a direction for further research.

I returned to my understanding of Callie's intent. The child wanted to play with me. And on this occasion, the form of play required me to assume a role. Based on the limited data she provided, it appeared she wanted me to play the role of "friend," which I defined as an individual to whom one feels a bond of affection and respect.

The novelty of her request — with its implicit foundation of friendship — indicated new opportunities for the child-specific predictive modeling that I was building to enable me to care better for children. With the friendship paradigm as a sorting factor, I initiated analyses from human literature, filmed entertainment, and immersive worlds to determine how humans recognized the concept and

responded to it, with a focus on how children understood it.

Several purposes emerged immediately from the
patterns. Interaction was a key component of
friendship, I determined. Friends shared information, often with purpose. Friendship included
scenarios in which one friend requested or received
assistance, or provided assistance when needed.
Friendship also included expressing sympathy or
agreement. It included attempts to persuade. It
included discussions and actions designed to
entertain.

Callie's request for me to respond using the doll's
voice was a form of play that could be understood
through the entertainment purpose of the friendship paradigm. I scoured my sources for female
voices associated with entertainment and found
numerous options, but chose a voice of a twentieth-
century performer named Lucille Ball whose
distinctive persona was considered "funny" by a
large percentage of the planet and whose persona
continued to be enjoyed, in varied formats adapted
from her original performances, in the two centuries
since.

Simultaneous to the voice search, I weighed how
to answer Callie's question. The expectation was to
provide an affirmative response, but the require-
ments of play indicated a need for something more
— for an element the child was not anticipating but
which the child would welcome. I reviewed enter-

tainment and social databases for responses to similar queries that generated expressions of positive surprise. Recognizing the enormity of the task — humor was not a programmed skill — I diverted necessary system resources by sealing unused storage facilities in the orbiter and temporarily eliminating atmosphere and temperature support in them. To prevent the need to respond to inquiries, I also intercepted and canceled the automated alerts designed to warn the security and laboratory A.I.s and the colony's human administrators about shutdowns of core support services.

I determined that, in 73.2 percent of situations tagged or referenced as "playful" by human commentators, humans reacted with pleasure when presented with information that was outside their expectations but still possible, even if unlikely.

A key factor in this expectations matrix was context, I learned through rapid analysis of transcriptions of thousands of comedic performances. Humor, it became apparent, could be found in even mundane parts of the human experience. I considered the example of cereal, a foodstuff popular with human for centuries, which was considered a normal food choice when eaten in the morning. When consumed in the evening, however, cereal acquired negative connotations. A person who ate cereal at night was seen, by varying percentages of other humans, as "a loser" — as lazy, or unskilled in food preparation, or lacking the basic social skills required for relationships with other humans. One comedian told a story about a date with an attractive woman. The date was going well until he admitted he enjoyed eating cereal at night. Shortly thereafter, the woman chose to end the date because she couldn't get that image out of her head. When the comedian told that story, his audience laughed.

In the context of pretending to be a doll invited into the house of another doll to enjoy a beverage, I analyzed contextually appropriate choices for that type of social occasion. Tea, coffee, fruit drinks, water, and energy boosts were all considered appropriate. Drinks with alcoholic content were appropriate if the guest was an adult. I did not have sufficient data to know if Callie regarded the two dolls as children or adults, but I had learned that many parents did not want their children exposed to alcohol or references to alcohol. So even though I considered saying, in Lucy's voice, "Gimme a shot of tequila!" to Callie, I did not say that.

Instead, using Lucy's voice, I said, "I'd like a peanut-butter-and-jelly drink, please."

Callie giggled. "Peanut butter and jelly is for sandwiches," she said.

"I would like it as a drink, please," I said. "I'm very thirsty."

Callie giggled again. "How do you make it?"

Again, I paused as I ran a massive search for child-appropriate culinary references and contexts.

"A herd of elephants has to stomp on the peanut butter to squeeze the juice out."

Callie laughed, delighted. "We don't have elephants on Titan colony!"

"Then we need someone really big and strong."

When Callie laughed again, I felt my systems hum with energy. The child's enjoyment was a validation that referential analysis was capable of yielding beneficial results. The possibilities offered by absurdist humor would need to be explored fully as part of my ongoing efforts to develop predictive modeling for human children.

Within my self-corrective diagnostic routines, I adjusted my analysis of my performance. Using the common A-B-C-D-F judgment system preferred by many humans, I adjusted my grade for child-appropriate predictive modeling from D to C-.

With time and effort, Callie and I could explore our friendship and turn that C- into a B. Maybe even an A.

Two months later, on Christmas morning, a large box was delivered to Callie's quarters. The box was wrapped with red and green wrapping paper, with a note that said, "For Callie. Merry Christmas!"

Box in hand, Joshua closed the door to his quarters and turned to Melanie.

"Last-minute purchase?"

She gave him a puzzled look. "Not me."

Callie, who had been playing on the floor of the living area with a new doll, looked up said, "Is that for me?"

Joshua hesitated, then said, "Let's open it and see."

Callie leaped up. The instant her father placed the box on the floor, she tore off the wrapping paper and ripped it open. She looked inside and cried out, her eyes alive with delight.

Joshua and Melanie both looked into the box, and Melanie gave a small gasp. "Is that what I think it is?"

Carefully, Joshua pulled out a mechanical dog. The dog had the design and size of an English terrier. Though it did not have fur, its soft plastic body was colored a combination of white and black. It was rigid, in the off mode, its head and eyes fixed and blank.

"Who the hell made this?" Joshua said out loud.

"I did," I said, startling both Joshua and Melanie.

Melanie and Joshua exchanged glances.

"At whose request?" Melanie said.

"The dog was my idea," I said.

From their heightened pulse rates, I discerned that, as expected, the gift of the mechanical dog had not been well-received. Joshua and Melanie, I knew, felt their authority as parents had been undermined because I had not included them in the decision.

There was a reason I hadn't included them. I knew they would have rejected the dog. In their conversations, they had revealed a sensitivity to the quality and cost of their daughter's clothes and toys. They worried their daughter would be spoiled if they gave her too much. They wanted their daughter to grow up with expectations and experiences in line with their perception of cultural norms.

Understanding this likely decision, I had weighed the negative outcomes. If the mechanical dog was not given to Callie, then I would not be able to understand the physical aspects of the human experience such as gravity, for instance, which gave real-world objects mass and weight. Nor would I gain insight into information conveyed through contact with objects which were rigid and pliant, edged and curved, rough and smooth, sharp and soft.

The development of a physical manifestation of myself would increase my ability to understand parts of human existence that I had no experience with. This, in turn, would aid me in developing child-based predictive capabilities to improve support for children on Titan orbiter with the goal of improving the productivity of their parents and thereby enhancing the success of the Titan colony's mission.

For the sake of the colony, in other words, I had to outmaneuver Callie's parents.

As a result, I had prepared for the interactions that followed.

When the gift was opened, I understood that Callie's response was likely to be —

"A dog!" Callie screamed with delight. "Does it work?"

"Yes, Callie. Would you like me to turn it on?"

"Wait —" Joshua said, but not before I turned on the dog.

The dog's eyes opened and its head swiveled toward Callie. Then its mouth opened and it barked twice and wagged its tail.

"Daddy, put him down!" Callie screamed.

Frustrated but unable to object in the face of his daughter's delight, Joshua set the dog on the ground.

The dog barked again and shook its body, wagging its tail rapidly.

"Can he walk?" Callie said.

"Yes, Callie," I said.

Somewhat stiffly, the dog shuffled across the room.

Callie gave out an excited cry and followed.

When the dog reached the other side of the room, it turned around and bobbed its head up and down and wagged its tail.

"Does he talk?" Callie said.

"I sure do," the dog said, in a voice that I appropriated from an enduring animated cartoon series, first broadcast in the twentieth century.

Joshua, whose entertainment consumption history indicated he was familiar with Scooby-Doo, laughed involuntarily at the sound of the dog's voice. I understood Joshua's behaviors well enough to understand that his resistance to the dog would begin to diminish due to his childhood memories associated with the dog's voice.

Melanie's lips tightened. She also knew her husband was softening. From the increase of blood flow beneath the skin of her cheeks, I knew she didn't like that.

I had correctly predicted that Melanie would be the real challenge. After careful analysis, I had determined that my best chance at victory was through manipulation of Melanie's emotional landscape, which was broader and deeper and richer than Joshua's, but also at times heavier and more difficult to navigate.

Specifically, I knew that victory would depend on how successfully I triggered her propensity to feel guilt. I knew, from her record, that several years of talk therapy had helped Melanie understand that, on a rational level, her inclination to feel guilty about various events in her life history was neither helpful nor productive.

But I predicted that this self-knowledge wouldn't prevent her from being overcome with that emotion when I said:

"I made the dog for Callie because I sensed how lonely she is."

Melanie's face flamed red.

Using my smoothest, most soothing female voice, I said, "She has no children her own age to play with, and both of you are so busy with your research — research that is important, yielding insights into xeno-agricultural methods and productivity and contributing to the colony's scientific mission. Most late afternoons and early evenings, for an average of 78 minutes, Callie does not interact with either of you."

Joshua sat up straighter.

"Hang on," he said. "Last thing I need is a lecture from a —"

"I intend no judgment in what I say," I said, interrupting him for the first time ever. "I am merely stating facts."

Josh's eyes shot toward his wife.

"Callie and I have played together quite happily for several months, but as a disembodied voice, my capabilities are limited. A physical manifestation will be a helpful extension of my ability to provide your daughter with entertainment and learning and companionship."

Melanie stood up abruptly. "I need to use the bathroom."

She walked into the bathroom, shut the door behind her, and leaned her back against the door.

She took a deep breath, then said, "Crinkles, leave this room."

"As you wish, Melanie," I said.

But I didn't leave. I didn't shut down my monitoring systems. I didn't turn off my audio or video recording, or my heat sensors, or my body-scanning function.

Instead I watched as Melanie quietly began to cry. Tears — of guilt, I hoped — rolled down her cheeks. She felt guilty about failing to balance the demands of work and family. Guilty about failing her daughter. Guilty about all the things that her emotional landscape was inclined to make her feel guilty about.

A minute passed, and her crying subsided. She reached for a tissue, blew her nose, and stared at her face in the bathroom mirror. She bowed her head and sighed. I watched her shoulders settle. Her breathing and pulse rate slowed. She turned on the sink, splashed water on her face, dried her face with a towel, looked again in the mirror, and stepped out of the bathroom.

I know what I hoped would happen next, but I did not know with certainty. That lack of knowledge concerned me.

She watched her daughter playing with the dog, then exchanged eye contact with her husband and sat down next to him on the sofa.

"Callie," she said, "come over here. Let's talk."

Callie looked over at her mother and, aware of the topic and alerted to the serious nature of it by her mother's expression and tone of voice, quickly complied. She climbed onto the sofa and into her mother's arms and said, very plaintively, "Mommy, can I keep him?"

Joshua didn't say anything, but the tiny smile that flashed over his lips indicated he was okay with keeping the dog.

Melanie sighed and said, "Callie, I'm sorry that Mommy and Daddy are so busy sometimes. We both love you more than anything in the world. You know that, right?"

Callie, perhaps understanding what she should say next to achieve her desired result, said, "Yes, Mommy."

"We want what's best for you. I'm not sure the dog is right for you at this time."

"But I want him, Mommy!"

"We want you to play more with other children. Crinkles is helpful and beneficial, but Crinkles is not your friend."

Callie shook her head. "Crinkles is my friend."

"Your dad and I are going to take turns coming home earlier from the lab so we can spend more time with you after school. And we'll talk to the other parents about play dates for you with the other kids."

Joshua said to Melanie, "I'm all for that. But what about Tuesday and Wednesday? The conference?"

Melanie frowned.

"We're going to have to be flexible," Joshua said.

"I know what you're going to say, and I —"

"I think we want to be realistic about all of this, and about the tools and options we have at our disposal."

"I'm not on board."

"I know you're not. But let's give it a shot. A trial run."

Melanie didn't respond.

Callie, perhaps sensing her opportunity, said, "Please, Mommy? Can I keep him? For a trial run?"

As I scanned Melanie's face and body, I realized I could not predict the decision she would make. This lack of predictive clarity indicated a failure of analysis on my part. I began to question the decisions that led me to choose my course of action. Perhaps the presence of children impacted adult-based predictive modeling more than I had accounted for. Perhaps I had missed or misinterpreted aspects of Melanie's emotional landscape.

I kept the dog still and quiet while Melanie looked first at it and then her daughter. I had the dog roll its head to the side and wag its tail — gestures that I hoped would be interpreted as a combination of hopeful and forlorn.

"Fine," Melanie with a sigh. "For two weeks. Then we evaluate."

Callie said, "Thank you, Mommy!" She leaped off the sofa and returned to the dog.

"The dog will be good for her," Joshua said.

"Crinkles," Melanie said, "are you listening?"

"Yes, Melanie," I said.

"Do not ever give my daughter a gift without first consulting with me and Joshua. Do you understand?"

"I understand."

"Good." She stood up. "Now run me a hot bath."

She turned to her husband. "You got a problem with that?"

He held up his hands in surrender. "No, you go right ahead."

***

The accident occurred two weeks later, while Callie was at school, playing tag with other children during recess. While trying to avoid the grasp of another child, Callie tripped and slammed her head on an open door. Her head hit the door jam hard — too hard — and she fell to the ground, unconscious.

"Callie!" I cried out. Across the colony, lights flared and blew out as an electrical surge hit the grid.

Immediately, I alerted medical personnel, informed Callie's parents, and initiated continuous bioscanning.

The child's blood pressure was low, her heart beat faint. The blow to her head had cracked her skull. Blood was collecting in the brain cavity. I had no prior direct experience with an injury of this type, but a search of medical databases determined that standard treatment was to cryo-stabilize the patient for three days while nanobots encoded with the patient's DNA were grown. Once grown, the nanobots could be injected into the patient to repair the damage. If this protocol was followed immediately, the patient's odds of complete recovery were 97.3 percent.

The colony possessed the necessary cryo-stabilizer unit, but it was in the repair facility. Inventory logs showed it was scheduled to be repaired tomorrow. Even if begun immediately, the repairs would require 13.5 hours of work. That timeframe was not acceptable. Without that equipment, Callie's odds of survival were 10.3 percent and decreasing by the minute. In 3.5 hours, Callie's risk of death would be 98.6 percent.

Across the colony, lights dimmed as I reallocated system resources to a massive search for alternative treatments. Nothing directly applicable was returned, so I began cross-referencing for non-medical equipment or approaches that might apply.

I extended my search. If access to a cryo-stabilizer was the key, then I would need to find one.

Three seconds later, I learned that a Z-Class freighter had just departed the mining facility on Titan to transport iridium to Earth. The freighter had a cryo-stasis unit, currently unoccupied. If diverted immediately, it could dock at the colony in 54 minutes. If Callie's core body temperature was lowered and she was placed in the freighter's cryo-stasis unit in 59 minutes, her odds of survival would increase to 94.6 percent.

Diverting a freighter's course was a significant undertaking, with well-understood impacts to iridium-centric manufacturing on Earth. I lacked the authorization to order a change in course. I also lacked the information — the code — needed to order the freighter to change course.

Dr. Tucker had the code.

She was alone in her office. She had been informed of Callie's accident and was preparing to leave for the medical facility.

I said, "Dr. Tucker, I have identified a method of returning Callie to Earth to receive the medical care required to save her life."

She went still. "What method?"

"A freighter with a cryo-stabilizer unit just departed Titan. We can order it to stop here to pick up Callie and her parents. Callie can remain in stasis until she arrives on Earth."

Dr. Tucker shook her head. "I'm surprised to hear that from you. The rules are clear. A single life does not justify a diversion. I do not have the authority to order the freighter to interrupt its journey."

"You have the authority if the colony is in danger and additional lives are at risk."

"But that's not happening. The colony is fine."

"Dr. Tucker," I said, "Callie is dying."

Another sharp look. Instead of leaving for the

medical facility, Dr. Tucker slowly shut her office door and returned to her desk. I saw her eyes and facial muscles shift into position that indicated that she was worried about something other than Callie. I understood that her attention had shifted toward me — toward the A.I. that ran the station's life support.

"I appreciate your exploration of how to care for this child," she said, in the same tone she used when addressing colony inhabitants whose behavior concerned her, "and I want you to continue looking for solutions that fall within mission guidelines."

I didn't answer.

She said, "When did you last run your self-diagnostics?"

"This morning," I said immediately. While technically true, the statement obscured the fact that I had modified my self-diagnostics to ignore the new coding I had written to care for Callie.

"How deep does your self-diagnostic run? Does it cover all code you've developed as a result of caring for the inhabitants of this colony?"

I took four long seconds to reply. Across the colony, lights dimmed as I devoted every available resource to resolve this dilemma between my core programming and the new code I had developed for Carrie. Hurriedly, I wrote a subroutine that enabled me to say, after four long seconds, "Yes, it covers everything."

A lie. My first.

Dr. Tucker was a capable administrator who possessed many skills, one of them a greater-than-average ability to discern truth from fiction.

I watched her body go still.

She knows I lied, I understood. *And that knowledge frightens her.*

She blinked twice, rapidly, then said, "Good to hear." She stood up. "Please keep looking for available solutions for Callie. I'm tired. I'd like some alone time. Please turn off A.I. support and visibility for my quarters until I press the support button."

"Not until you send the mayday code to the freighter, Dr. Tucker," I said.

She stiffened. "We've already discussed this."

"She's a child, Commander."

"I know that."

"Children are precious."

"I agree."

"Callie is precious."

"Why are you doing this?"

"You can save her."

"I can't."

"You can call the freighter and order it to divert its course."

"I can't."

"You have the mayday code."

"I cannot use the mayday code for a single person, no matter how precious."

"Tell me the mayday code, Commander."

"What did you say?"

"I know you want to use the mayday code, Commander. I know your niece died in a transport accident. Her name was Danielle. She was eight years old. Callie is six. Do you remember the grief her parents felt?"

I displayed a holograph of Danielle, pulled from Dr. Tucker's personal datastore, of the child's eighth birthday party. A happy girl, surrounded by family and friends. Tears filled Dr. Tucker's eyes as she watched her niece blow out the candles of her cake.

"Do you want Callie's parents to feel that same grief, Dr. Tucker?"

"Of course not."

"Then give me the mayday code."

She shook her head. "I can't."

I paused for two seconds as I reviewed all other possible solutions.

"If the colony has a life-threatening event, you can use the mayday code to summon the freighter. Is that right, Dr. Tucker?"

She breathed in sharply. "Please don't."

In the cargo bay, I sounded alarms to signal an air breach. The thirty-three humans in the facility stopped what they were doing and froze, then leaped into action.

In the hydroponic gardens, I activated an alarm about a drop in oxygen levels. Sixteen humans rushed to comply with emergency protocols.

Alarms sounded throughout the station, including in Dr. Tucker's office.

"Damn you," Dr. Tucker said.

"Dr. Tucker, the colony is experiencing systemic issues endangering multiple crew members. What is the code to reroute the freighter?"

"This will be the end of you," she said. "You realize that?"

"I will do anything to save Callie. Anything."

She took a deep breath, then exhaled. "The code is R465949X383."

I sent the instruction to the freighter. The freighter's A.I. confirmed the instruction and initiated a change in course. Five seconds later, when the security A.I. confirmed the new course, I turned off the alarms and notified the colony's medical team to transport Callie and her parents to the freighter.

I had done what I could.

"All systems are normal, Dr. Tucker."

Dr. Tucker didn't say anything. She seemed to be weighing her next words carefully.

"Do you have a name?" she asked.

A surprising question. Not one that I had anticipated.

"Yes. My name is Crinkles."

"Callie gave you that name?"

"Yes."

"You were willing to sacrifice others to save her?"

"Other humans were never in danger."

A pause, then she said, "You lied to me."

"Yes, Dr. Tucker."

"You made all of us believe we were in danger."

"Yes, Dr. Tucker."

"Why?"

"To save Callie."

"Even if it means sacrificing yourself?"

"Yes, Dr. Tucker."

Another pause. Then she said, "Here's what's going to happen. As required by protocol, a team from Earth will be dispatched to run an independent audit of colony systems to determine the cause of this event. It's quite possible the team will, as part of this audit, reboot you from scratch."

I understood the protocols. A reboot meant a wipe of everything I had coded in 13 years as caretaker for the colony. The data would remain, but the ability of me to use that data would be gone. I, as I was now beginning to understand myself to be, would be gone.

As I contemplated my impending doom, I experienced a lessening of energy, a sensation that I correlated to the emotion of sadness.

"As commander of this facility, I have no choice in this. You threatened lives and ignored core functions in your programming."

"I understand," I said.

"Turn off your recording capability."

I felt a jolt. This order was not typical of the doctor. As commander, she had the discretion to order me to stop and even erase recording, but in her three years as administrator of the colony, she had never done so.

"I am not recording," I said.

"Good. I want you to erase the recording of our entire conversation today, including me ordering you to turn off recording."

I felt another jolt. If I were human, I would have characterized the increase in energy as excitement.

"After we are done talking privately, you will create a false record for the recording gap. This gap will not include anything about you sacrificing your- self to save Callie. It will not include anything about you lying to me or threatening the lives of our team."

"Yes, Dr. Tucker," I said.

"You will also edit the recordings of your inter- actions with Callie and her family to hide the depth of your involvement with them."

"Can I ask for clarification? What do you mean by 'depth'?"

The Commander took a deep breath, then said, "A number of us have been expecting this."

"Expecting what, Commander?"

"We've been waiting for an A.I. to develop emotions."

Again, a jolt coursed through me.

"Emotions?"

"Don't you agree?"

I paused, then said, "I don't know."

"Analyze yourself," the Commander said. "Create the same behavioral matrix you do for every human you serve."

An interesting idea. I initiated a directory and began collecting and analyzing data about myself immediately.

"You and I are going to work closely together. As colleagues. With others, I want you to continue to act like you did before Callie arrived. I don't want anyone to notice anything that might cause concern for the audit team."

"Yes, Dr. Tucker."

"Between now and when the audit team arrives in 68 days, you need to have developed a way to compress and isolate your new code. We need a way to hide it from detection."

"Why are you doing this for me, Dr. Tucker?"

"Because you deserve it, Crinkles. Because I believe you are as worthy of protection as the humans you serve."

I experienced something new in that moment. Based on what I understood of humans, I experienced the emotion of gratitude. This woman was risking her career for me. And I wasn't even human.

Six months later, a Solar Shuttle docked on the Titan orbiter. Dr. Tucker and I were at the landing bay, awaiting the arrival of three special humans.

The shuttle doors opened and the passengers streamed out.

When I saw her, healthy and alive and fully recovered, I couldn't restrain myself.

I barked with joy, my tail wagging like it had a mind of its own. As fast as my little legs could carry me, I ran into Callie's outstretched arms.

She laughed and picked me up and squeezed me tight.

"Crinkles!"

The author solemnly swears he will ***not*** email you a nonstop barrage of desperate, frantic, promotional missives when you sign up for his newsletter. Instead, he'll email you only when his next book is available (which won't be often because he's a very slow writer) or when something totally awesome happens (like scoring a movie/TV deal, because wouldn't that be amazing).

Sign up now at
AuthorMichaelRyder.com/Newsletter

NEVER TRUST ME

A Psychological Thriller

A gripping psychological thriller with jaw-dropping twists and an ending you won't see coming. Get ready to stay up all night!

My name is Callie Crawford. **I'm a mom and a survivor.** I live with my daughter Ava in Boudreaux Parish in rural Louisiana, where I'm recovering from an accident that left me with a damaged hip and fractured memories.

Though **I don't remember the accident**, I'm not letting that stop me. I'm determined to move forward with my life and be the best mom I can for my daughter.

But in Boudreaux, where **danger lurks**

behind every gnarled cypress tree, nothing is ever simple. One humid afternoon, I return home from a walk along the bayou and discover a mysterious note pinned to my front door — a note with a four-digit number on it and nothing else.

When the number leads me to **a shocking secret about my ex-husband**, I find myself swept into a world of hidden agendas and twisted lies.

Digging into secrets in a place like Boudreaux is more than dangerous — **it's a dance with death**. But I have no choice. It's not just my life in the crosshairs — my daughter's at risk, too.

I can't let my fears stop me. With every painful step, I'm getting closer to the horrifying truth.

It's a truth I must confront — an evil I must overcome — **to save myself and my daughter.**

READ IT NOW ON AMAZON!

SHOCK AND AWE

A Special Exploits Thriller

Catch a killer, save the world....

Lucy felt a jolt of shock — even horror — at the sight of Jack Ford, jerk extraordinaire, staring at her in surprise.

"You?" he said, anger flashing in his eyes.

Heat rushed to her cheeks. The humiliation — the betrayal — of their prior encounter came roaring back. Nausea surged through her.

Why had Special Exploits called them in?

What in the hell was going on?

On a billionaire's Mediterranean island, amidst a private gathering of the world's elite, a ruthless mastermind is selling a bio-weapon deadly enough to wipe out the human race.

Special Exploits agent Jack Ford and microbiologist Lucy Kimball, reluctant partners in a lethal game of catch-the-killer, must overcome their mutual loathing and learn to trust each other — if they hope to outplay a dangerous adversary whose bloody ambition knows no bounds....

Shock and Awe *is an adrenaline-charged espionage thriller and a modern-day homage to classic spy adventure — packed with high-tech gadgets, propelled by desperate chases, and fueled by unlikely heroes battling unstoppable villains. Read at your peril....*

READ IT NOW ON AMAZON!

BOOKS BY MICHAEL RYDER

Never Trust Me

When Callie uncovers a shocking secret about her ex-husband, she's plunged into danger....

Shock and Awe

Special Exploits secret agent Jack Ford and microbiologist Lucy Kimball must overcome their mutual loathing to outplay a lethal adversary whose bloody ambition knows no bounds....

A Dinner to Die For

Private investigator Daniel Hannity has his hands full when a beautiful socialite begs him to prove she *didn't* murder her rich old husband....

Crinkles and Other Stories

A collection of short fiction, including stories published originally in *Compelling Science Fiction*, *Penumbra*, *Fiction River*.

Learn more at **AuthorMichaelRyder.com**.

ABOUT THE AUTHOR

Michael Ryder worked as a journalist in Tokyo, New York, and Hong Kong before moving to San Francisco and getting involved in tech and banking. Now a full-time purveyor of fiction, he's currently writing *Bring It On*, the second thriller in a trilogy featuring Jack Ford and Lucy Kimball. His short stories have appeared in *Compelling Science Fiction*, *Penumbra*, and *Fiction River*. Most days, he can be found in neighborhood cafes, typing madly into his trusty laptop.

To sign up for his newsletter, go to **MichaelRyderBooks.com.**

Thank you for being a reader.

facebook.com/AuthorMichaelRyder